The Four Little Children

9/7/11

To Nick —

Enjoy these adventure
with my Children !
Your Friend —
Larry Nicholson

from Nick —

The Four Little Children

A Likely Story

Written 1970–1971
Compiled 1986
Illustrated 2007

Larry Michalove

iUniverse, Inc.
New York Lincoln Shanghai

The Four Little Children
A Likely Story

iUniverse books may be ordered through booksellers or by contacting:

iUniverse
2021 Pine Lake Road, Suite 100
Lincoln, NE 68512
www.iuniverse.com
1-800-Authors (1-800-288-4677)

Because of the dynamic nature of the Internet, any Web addresses or links contained in this book may have changed since publication and may no longer be valid.

This is a work of fiction. All of the characters, names, incidents, organizations, and dialogue in this novel are either the products of the author's imagination or are used fictitiously.

ISBN: 978-0-595-34799-5 (pbk)
ISBN: 978-0-595-67157-1 (cloth)
ISBN: 978-0-595-79534-5 (ebk)

Printed in the United States of America

The kindergarten class of Sarah Michalove (granddaughter of author) listened intently to and thoroughly enjoyed the reading of Mr. Michalove's stories. They were awesome character-building stories, during which the class asked many questions and learned about love, respect, and responsibility.

Mrs. Mary Schmidt, kindergarten teacher
East Side Elementary School
Marietta, Georgia

To My Wife,
Sybil

Contents

Introduction

In July 1970, I moved my family to Birmingham, Alabama, in anticipation of a pending navigation assignment to the 16th Special Operations Squadron (AC-130 gunships) in Ubon, Thailand. Our mission would be to stop nightly truck traffic moving down the Ho Chi Minh Trail in Laos. Ultimately I flew 114 night combat missions, receiving two Distinguished Flying Crosses and nine Air Medals. The more difficult assignment fell to my wonderful wife, best friend, and companion, Sybil. It was her role to continue raising our "four little children," Lisa, David, Stacy, and Karen, ages nine, six and a half, two and three-quarters, and one and a half, respectively.

On a hot July third in 1970, I moved my family into a three-bedroom apartment in the Homewood, Alabama, area, a suburb of Birmingham. We won't forget that day, as the air-conditioning in the apartment did not work, and the temperature exceeded a scorching 100 degrees Fahrenheit. My departure date for the Vietnam conflict was mid-November. Between July and November, I was to complete combat crew training at Lockbourne Air Force Base, Ohio; Air Force survival school training at Fairchild Air Force Base, Washington; and jungle survival school near Clark Air Base in the Philippines. With these training assignments added to my Vietnam tour, I spent about fourteen months away from my family. The survival schools were difficult and depressing, as I went through them not knowing if I would ever see my family again. I learned somewhat how to survive under difficult circumstances, but, even more, I had firmly implanted in my mind the thought, "Don't get captured in the first place."

I will never forget boarding the airplane in Birmingham for departure to the late fall survival school in Washington state. I looked back over my shoulder to see Sybil standing there, crying on my mother's shoulder. I will never forget calling Sybil from the terminal of Travis Air Force Base in California, where I was awaiting my flight to the Philippines. It was difficult to hear, because the terminal was very noisy, and ironically, Peter, Paul, and Mary were singing the tune "Leaving on a Jet Plane" over a jukebox. I remember telling Sybil good-bye with a tremendous lump in my throat. All of these things happened sixteen years ago, and I will never forget them.

During my time away, I included in letters to Sybil stories that she could read to our children. I felt that they would be thrilled to read of adventures that included themselves as the primary characters. Fortunately, Sybil saved all of my letters, which after these many years, I have finally compiled.

Those times were much more difficult for Sybil than for me. She had to raise four little children and worry about me, too. It was even harder for her, because she was living in a civilian environment where most people's contact with the Vietnam conflict was to read about it in the papers or watch the protests on television. She worried about losing a husband. Family, a few close friends, and the nightly news got her through a difficult time in our lives.

Participation in the Vietnam conflict is like other things that I have done in my life—I'm glad that I did it, but I wouldn't want to do it again.

Larry Michalove
1986

July 1970
Karen, one and a half; David, six and a half; Lisa, nine; and Stacy, two and
three-quarters.

The Four Little Children
A Likely Story

Well, kids, knowing how much you like stories, and since I am far away and you are way back there in Alabama, I thought that I would write exciting stories for your mom to read to you. This would be the next best thing to my being at home telling them to you myself.

As usual, our story begins with a "Once upon a time." And, it so happens, that this story, as in our old stories, has four little children named (you guessed it) Lisa (age nine), David (age six), Stacy (age two and three-quarters), and Karen (age one and a half). They were good little children who always obeyed their mother and father. One day, they were sitting around the house with nothing to do (it was a rainy Saturday), so they decided to put on their nice, shiny raincoats, sneak out an umbrella, and take a lovely stroll through the woods to pick wildflowers for their pretty mother. They also hoped to have fun chasing the squirrels and chipmunks along the way.

Lisa and David were in the lead, with little Stacy and Karen holding hands and trailing along behind. All four children started off down the path picking wildflowers and putting them into a straw basket, which they had brought from home. Lisa and David took turns holding the basket, because as it started filling with flowers, it became a little on the heavy side—too heavy for little Karen to hold! They collected green flowers, yellow flowers, blue flowers, big flowers, and little flowers. All of the flowers were for their mother, who was at home making cakes and pies for her precious children.

It was getting on toward lunchtime, so Lisa decided it was time to eat. She had made jelly sandwiches and cheese sandwiches to bring, along with cookies, pickles, and apples. She spread them out neatly on a tablecloth for their lunch. She and David had risen early that morning and gathered all of these things together for their outing. They had even made a great big jar of lemonade. The picnic was set under the shade of a large oak tree, which was located on a soft, mossy bank, not too far from a little stream. The rain had cleared up, and blue sky was beginning to show through the clouds. The children ate all their lunch—not one crumb was left—and then lay down on the mossy slope to take a little nap.

They slept soundly in the warm, afternoon sun with full tummies and dreamed of candy canes, sailing ships, baby dolls, and all sorts of wonderful things. David even dreamed about a little dog that he wanted. Well, it so happens that they slept much later than they had planned. Lisa awoke with a start and realized that the sun was beginning to set, and it was time to go home. Lisa had her watch on, but it had stopped. All she knew was that it must be getting late, and that Mother would be wondering where she and David had wandered with those babies. She woke David, and the two of them looked around to see where the babies had gone. They were nowhere to be seen. They began shouting, "Stacy, Karen, where are you?"

No one answered!

Since the ground was still damp from the rain, David thought they might find footsteps on the path near where they had slept. Sure enough he saw footsteps leading down the path into the dark forest. Lisa and David started to run. Their fear was soon put to rest, as they came upon their little sisters playing in the grass and sliding down a small hill in the meadow. Alas, the children were a mess, with dirt and grass stains all over their pretty dresses. Lisa and David had to laugh. They were such a silly sight to behold. Lisa and David took the babies down to the stream and washed them, and then the children headed for home as fast as they could go.

When they arrived home, Mother asked where they had been. Lisa told her of their afternoon stroll, and it was then that the two baby sisters surprised Mother with the beautiful basket of flowers they had collected. Mother was pleased with the flowers. She let the children help her arrange them in a bowl. They looked mighty pretty sitting on the dining room table.

That night while they were in bed, David said to Lisa, "Let's go back to that same spot tomorrow. I'm certain there was something very peculiar about that place that I've just got to check out."

"What was that?" asked Lisa.

"Well," said David, "there was a big rock behind that oak tree with an *X* on it. When I woke up and we ran after the babies, I forgot all about it. We've got to go back and investigate. It seemed very mysterious to me!"

It was time to go to sleep, and they did just that. Soon they would dream of going to investigate the mysterious *X* on the big rock that David had seen earlier in the day.

Skull and Crossbones

As you know, all four children made it home safe and sound after their last trip into the woods. David, however, had seen a mysterious rock in the woods that had a funny-looking X on it. He felt that they should definitely go back together and investigate that mysterious-looking rock. Of course, Lisa and David had school all week, and Mother wouldn't let the babies go roaming around the woods by themselves. The fall days were getting dark very early in the evening, so there just wasn't much daylight left in which the children could go exploring after school. Each day when they came home from school, Lisa and David would gather with their little sisters and make plans for their adventure to find the mysterious rock. They were hoping so much that it wouldn't rain Saturday morning and spoil their fun.

This time they made plans very carefully and even drew out a little map so they would be sure to find the place where David had seen the mysterious rock. David was now old enough to carry a pocketknife. He thought he would take his new knife along to mark the trees, so they wouldn't lose their way. He had read a book in school about Indian scouts and how they had done just that.

By Friday night the children were much too excited about their upcoming adventure to go to sleep. All four of them curled up on Lisa's bed and talked about plans for the next day. Lisa and Stacy would get up early and pack a lunch for everyone while David would help little Karen get dressed. They would all put on play clothes and get up earlier than usual this Saturday morning. Finally, they fell asleep in Lisa's room, and Mother had to carry them to their own beds. (I don't see how she managed to carry such big children.)

Well, early the next morning the big adventure began. When Mother awoke that morning there they were—all four of them— standing beside her bed with bright shining faces. "What are you children doing up so early?" she asked.

"We thought we would go out to play," they replied in unison.

"Well, OK," she said. "I'll get up and fix a nice breakfast of pancakes for everyone."

Everyone pitched in and helped to set the breakfast table, and in no time they were licking their lips and rubbing full tummies. What a good breakfast they had eaten.

"So long, Mom," they cried.

"Aren't you children going to watch cartoons this morning?"

"No," they replied. "We think we'll take a nice walk in the woods."

"Be careful," Mother said. "Make sure that you come home before dark. I see that you are taking your lunch, so have a nice picnic. I'll be looking for you later on this afternoon."

They scampered out of the house and over to the edge of the woods. With his map in hand, David led the way. Lisa thought it would be a good idea to keep Stacy and Karen in the middle, so they wouldn't straggle behind. She brought up the rear. They went down the path, taking their time to enjoy the warm, morning sun. They decided to sing songs and sang aloud as they walked.

Once they saw a cute, little bunny rabbit hop across their path, but he wasn't around long enough to be very sociable. Birds were singing in the trees, and, all in all, it was just a grand day. The children were having fun as they strolled. In the meantime, David was studying his map. Soon they came upon a big rock beside the path, but this wasn't their rock. David knew that just around the next bend he would soon find the tree that marked the spot where he had seen his mysterious rock.

He remembered the tree, because it was a big oak tree, and there were quite a few acorns lying on the ground around it. He had picked up one of the acorns, cut the top off, hollowed it out, and then stuck a little stick into one end. He had fashioned a cute little pipe, and the girls had gathered around to see what he had made. He had put it in his pocket and thought that one day he would give it to his dad.

Finally, they came upon the towering oak tree. They went behind the big tree, and David stood there scratching his head. "Where did I see that funny-looking rock?" David wondered out loud. "Oh yes, it was over behind that big clump of grass."

They went over, and Stacy was the first to spot the shiny rock with the *X* on it. Lisa gingerly picked it up. It glistened in the sunlight and had small shiny streaks running all through it.

"I'm sure this rock must be made of gold," Lisa said, "and these shiny things in it are precious jewels— perhaps diamonds and rubies, but probably only flecks of mica."

She just couldn't understand the meaning of the big red *X* that was marked on one side. Suddenly Lisa said, "I believe I know what this means!" They all looked at Lisa and awaited her explanation with great anticipation. "In one of my mystery books, there was a story about a secret hiding place marked with an *X*. In the book they said, '*X* marks the spot.' I'll bet that is just what it means here! The *X* on our rock is marking this spot for something very special."

David suggested they should dig where the rock was lying, and perhaps they would find a clue.

Then they heard Stacy's stomach growl. Lisa decided they should eat lunch now, because everyone seemed to be getting hungry. This time no one would take a nap after lunch. They didn't want to over-sleep and wished to get on with their digging as soon as possible.

After lunch they found several sticks and began moving the soil upon which the rock had been lying. The soil was soft and loosely packed, so they were easily able to scoop it out of the way. Soon a big hole began to develop. Just then they heard a "thump, thump," when little Karen's stick hit something hard. It was a black- and silver-colored box. Lisa reached down carefully to pick it up. It was covered with dirt and moss and looked very, very old. She opened it. Inside was a black flag with a white skull and crossbones on it.

"I know what that is," David exclaimed. "It's a pirate's flag!" And it was just that! Suddenly, a very old piece of rolled-up, yellowed paper fell out of the flag and gently floated down upon the grass.

Lisa picked it up and began to read it to herself. "Wow!" she exclaimed. "Look at this!"

The Little Man

We last left those four children all excited when they found the buried pirate's flag. As you remember, an unusual piece of paper dropped to the ground as the flag unrolled. Lisa picked it up.

"What does it say?" the others excitedly exclaimed!

She read it aloud to them. "Hmm," she wondered aloud. "What does this mean?" She thought for a moment and then said to her brother and sisters, "Well, I'm not sure. It must be in some sort of magic code. You look at it, David."

She put the paper on the ground, and they gathered round to see what the message said. They saw these confusing words written on the paper:

S'etarip Cigam,
Ot Uoy Ruof, Fi Uoy
Tsuj Yas, "Romar."

David had recently learned to read, and even he couldn't make out what it said. "We're just going to have to figure this thing out for ourselves," Lisa said. "I know that it must be an important message! What do you think we ought to try first, David?"

"Well, maybe if we held it up to a mirror, we could see a message reflected in the words," he suggested. David had once read about doing that in one of his magic books.

Lisa happened to have a small mirror with her, because she liked to make sure her face wasn't dirty after she played, and she held the old paper up to it. But it just didn't seem to work. "It still doesn't make sense to me," she said. "Stacy, you hold up the paper, and I'm going to take a stick and copy the words over again in the dirt. But this time I'm going to write each word down backwards."

She began, and the more words she wrote down, the more excited she became. Here's what she found out:

> Pirate's Magic,
> To You Four, If You
> Just Say, "Ramor."

She read it aloud to the children. They wondered about the Pirate's Magic and just what this message meant.

David suggested that they say the magic word, "Ramor," together, and perhaps something might happen. He counted to three, and they all chimed together, "Ramor!" All of a sudden, there was a blinding flash of light and a large puff of smoke. The pirate's flag had disappeared, and the rock with the X on it was also gone. Standing in their place was a small, jolly, little man with a snow-white beard just like Santa Claus's. "Don't be frightened, my little children," he said. "I am your friend. I have been waiting here a long time for you to find me."

Karen and Stacy were a little frightened at first and were hiding behind Lisa and David. But the little man seemed so friendly and looked so jolly that none of the children were really afraid of him for very long.

David asked him, "How did you know we were coming? Are you some sort of an elf? Are you magic?"

"Why are you here?" Lisa added.

In the meantime, Karen and Stacy wandered over to the little man and sat down beside him. They seemed to sense that he was some sort of special friend.

The little man replied, "First, let me say that my name is Ramor, and the reason I am here is that you called me. Of course, I knew you were going to call, and I was just waiting. You are right, David. I am magic, and I am a very special kind of elf. I have been sent from the land of good fairies to watch over you children while your father is far away. As you will see, very special things happen to very special children, and you are very special children. I will take you to many places, and we will see and do many strange and exciting things together. I have a magic carpet we will ride, high into the sky. While you are with me, you will have certain magic powers, too. Nothing can harm you. You will be able to fly through the rain with me and not get wet; we can walk among people and animals, and they won't see us or hear us unless we want them to. We are going to have many wonderful adventures together. What do you think about that?"

All of the children were very excited about the thought of such magnificent adventures, however, Lisa and David didn't think that their mom would let them go wandering all over the world like that.

Lisa spoke up. "Ramor, I don't think that our mother would let us be gone from home for such a long time. Besides, we have school, and many other things that have to be done. It would be wonderful, but I just don't think that we can go."

"It won't be difficult at all, children," Ramor replied. "You see, you forget that this will be a magic journey. Each day we can travel many places and have our adventures, and even though it might seem a long time, you will only be gone for a short while or some-times maybe just a little longer. It will almost be like a dream. All you have to do is come to this secret spot by the oak tree near the stream and say my name, and I will come to you. Remember that I am your special friend and will look out for you and take care of you while you are with me. Tonight I will explain to your mother while she dreams who I am and about all the wonderful things we are going to do together. Right now, I want you children to hurry home and help your mother with supper and the other chores around the house. The next time you come back here, we will begin our first adventure, and you four will come with me on a magical trip to seek a pirate's treasure. See you soon!"

With that, he disappeared in the same blinding flash of light that had occurred when he had first appeared.

First Adventures

When the children arrived home it was around four o'clock in the afternoon and they would soon be getting ready for dinner. The girls were busily helping in the kitchen, setting the table. David was in his room putting up the toy cars with which the little girls had been playing earlier in the day. Everyone was hungry and looked forward to dinner. When they were at the table and passing food around, Mother asked, "Well children, what did you do this afternoon? Did you have a good time on your walk?"

Lisa looked at David, and they both had big grins on their faces. They didn't know whether to tell Mom about their special little man or not.

Stacy piped up and said, "We met a funny little man in the woods today."

"You know that you children aren't supposed to talk to strangers," Mother said. "What did he say?"

Lisa and David began to relate the afternoon's adventures. Mother said that it all sounded very strange to her.

"He indeed sounds like a very special guardian angel for you children, but I have only heard of that sort of thing happening in books and fairy tales. I'll have to think about it tonight, and I'll discuss it with you again at breakfast before you go to school."

The dinner dishes were cleaned in a flash, and Lisa and David hurried to their rooms to play, while Mother read Stacy and Karen a story about Bozo the clown. Everyone was eager for Mother to go bed that night, for they knew that Ramor would come to her in a dream and assure her that his adventures with her children would be all right.

The next thing Mother knew, it was 7:30 PM, and the children had already dressed in their pajamas all by themselves and said they were ready for bed. Mother tucked everyone in and kissed each of them good night. After a while, she too began to get sleepy and decided to climb into her bed.

In the meantime Lisa, David, Stacy, and Karen were keeping their fingers crossed that their mother would have a very special dream that night. And what do you know? She did.

At breakfast the next morning, all the children kept asking their mother how she had slept the night before.

"Well," she said, "you were right, and that friend of yours, Ramor, must truly be magic. While I was sleeping, this short little man who looked like Santa Claus came to me in my dream and explained how he was going to watch over you children and take you on marvelous adventures. I think it will be all right, and I'm sure that your dad would say OK if he were here. He'd probably want to share the adventures with you."

Stacy chimed in, "That's the little man all right. He sure was nice and jolly. I like him and so does Karen."

Well, that settled that, and the big kids were off to school. They both came home promptly that afternoon, because they were ready to get started on their search for Ramor and the pirate's treasure that he had promised them. Hand in hand, all four children strolled down the path into the woods looking for the big oak tree beside the stream. It was a clear, cold afternoon, and everyone had on jackets. The few leaves remaining on the trees were vivid shades of red and gold but most had fallen to the ground. Cold weather had set in early this year. Every now and then, a squirrel or chipmunk would scamper across their path. The birds were still singing in the trees, and generally it was just a wonderful day.

They arrived at their spot beside the oak tree (it was only about a thirty minute walk from home) and sat down to rest.

David said, "I think we should all stand up and call Ramor together."

"Good idea," replied Lisa. "I'm ready for our adventure. It's going to be so exciting! I just want it to begin!"

All four of the children stood up, and, at the top of their voices, they shouted, "Ramor! Ramor! Ramor!"

No sooner than you could snap your fingers, there was a puff of smoke, and there he was, their special little man. "Here I am, children. I was just waiting for you to arrive. Shall we go?"

Everyone shouted yes in unison. They followed him behind the tree, and there they saw a beautifully woven carpet lying before them on the ground. The magic carpet was shades of red and gold and shimmered in the sunlight, so much so that it looked almost like a ray of sunlight itself. It was just about the size of their mother's bed, perhaps a little larger. There was room enough for all four children and Ramor to sit comfortably upon it.

"Here we go children, high into the sky," said Ramor. "Don't be afraid. You cannot fall off. Remember, when you are with me, you have special powers."

With that, they zoomed straight up into the sky. They could look down on the tops of trees, and at all of the houses and apartments. The cars looked like little toys, and the houses seemed no bigger than Stacy's blocks. The children were thrilled. Higher and higher they went up into the clouds, and before long they were looking down at the birds. The children were amazed at the sights that they were seeing. The carpet climbed over high mountains, and they could see the green forests below. Soon, out in the distance they spotted a gigantic lake. But wait, no, it wasn't a lake; they had flown all the way to the Pacific Ocean. They were going down a little lower now and could see palm trees and white sandy beaches. The carpet then made a sharp turn, and they were now looking into the mouth of a deserted cave along the water's edge.

There in one corner of the cave was an old sailing ship. It didn't look very big from up high, but the closer they got, the bigger the ship became. They could also see several people on the beach. The people at first looked like little ants, but they, too, became more recognizable and bigger as the carpet came closer to the ground.

"We'll just hover here for a while and watch what is going on below," said Ramor.

David asked, "Doesn't that ship have a pirate's flag on the mast?"

"Yes," answered Ramor. "Those are real pirates down there, and if you look closely you will see that they have a big trunk with them, and it is filled with precious jewels. They are digging a hole in the sand in which to hide their treasure and will someday come back here to this very spot and take their treasure away with them. In just a little while, we are going to join them. Hang on tight, kids. Here we go!"

The Secret Cave

The magic carpet began to get lower and lower, and the children could see more clearly what was happening on the beach below. They could see several men, and sure enough they looked like pirates. One man had a black patch over one eye and even had a wooden leg. He had a great big, shiny sword at his side and a colorful parrot standing on his shoulder. He appeared to be the leader of the group. Ramor said for the children not to be worried, because he was a personal friend of the pirate chief, and besides that, with their magical powers, nothing could hurt them anyway.

The pirate chief looked up into the sky at the magic carpet. He had to hold his hands over his eyes to shade them from the bright sunlight. He immediately recognized Ramor and waved to him. The carpet came in for a gentle landing on the sandy beach, and the children could see that four of the pirates were digging a large hole. There was a great big pirate's chest beside it. The pirate leader's name was Aranal, and he came over to greet Ramor and the children.

"I see that you have brought your little friends to visit, Ramor. We will show them the ways of the pirates!" he enthusiastically exclaimed.

Now, as you know, all pirates are not necessarily bad men. Some are a happy, adventurous lot. These were good pirates, and they tried to live in peace and help their fellow man.

"Let us finish burying our treasure, and then I will take you to our ship," Aranal said. "Later we will sail to a very special place."

Aranal opened the treasure chest and showed the children the gold and magnificent jewels that were inside. The children were amazed at the sparkle and glitter of everything. The pirate explained that this was just a small treasure to confuse people who might come to take the pirates' precious jewels. If someone found this treasure, perhaps they would stop looking and leave without finding the main treasure.

Aranal signaled for the children to come with him. They followed him down the beach toward the water where the boat was docked. The children were very excited to see the big ship with three tremendous white sails rising high into the sky. It was even more exciting when the ship set sail toward the mysterious mountains. One of the smallest pirates said, "David, come with me," and together they began to climb the rigging up to a little lookout stand called "the crow's nest." When David got to the top, the little pirate gave him a spyglass to look through, and David could see for miles around. Now he could better see the distant, ominous-looking mountains, which in a way reminded him of the accordion-like, volcanic mountains that his dad had once shown him when they lived in Hawaii.

When they came down, Aranal said to David, "Did you see the dark mountains to the east? In those mountains is located the cave of the pirates. That's where our families live and where we keep our most precious possessions."

The ship itself was very clean, and was made of beautiful, shiny wood. Someone said it was made mostly of teakwood and mahogany. One of the pirates brought out a platter of fruit for the children to eat. The pirate also had a cute little gibbon monkey on his shoulder for them to play with. The monkey mischievously hopped onto Stacy's shoulder, and she made friends with it right away. Karen was busy eating a banana, when suddenly the monkey jumped over to her and took a piece of it. Everyone laughed, and little Karen thought it was funny, too.

After they had an opportunity to thoroughly explore the ship, the pirate chief gathered them together and said, "We have arrived! It is time to march to the mountains!"

Everyone marched down the gangplank and onto the trail that led along the beach, into the jungle, and then to the dark mountains. When they at last arrived at the mountaintop, four of the strongest pirates pushed a large stone aside, and there was the entrance to a large cave, which led into the side of the mountain. Inside, the air was cool, and they heard the rush of water in the distance. They saw the glitter of jewels strewn along the sides of the cave, and there were torches along the walls to light their way. Finally they came to an underground stream. Several small boats were tied up along the bank. Lisa and David both thought this seemed just like Disneyland's "Pirates of the Caribbean," so it had to be real. They climbed into the boats, and down the rushing river they went. They came out into a little city on the other side of the mountain. The streets were clean, there were many kinds of colorful flowers growing, and several children quickly came over to greet Lisa, David, Stacy, and Karen.

"Now," said Aranal, "I'll take you to see what no one but the pirates has ever seen before."

Back into the cave they went. They came upon several pirate guards, but when they saw that the children were with Aranal, they let them pass. They entered a room in the cave that was bigger than their whole apartment. It was filled with unusual gold coins, diamonds, rubies, emeralds, and all sorts of other precious gems. The children were astounded at this magnificent display. They had never before seen so many jewels.

"Is this the precious treasure that you said you were going to show us?" the children asked.

Aranal responded, "You have already seen our most precious treasure; that was our healthy children, happily playing with one another. True, this treasure of gold and jewels is worth much money, but nothing is more valuable to us than our children."

Lisa said, "I know our parents feel the same way as you do, Aranal."

"Now," said the pirate, "you may take one jewel home with you for your beautiful mother to enjoy."

There was so much to choose from, but the children finally picked out one pretty, sparkling diamond. The diamond they chose was a clear gem, a symbol of piety, beauty, and kindness.

Finally Ramor said, "Now children, you have seen the pirate's treasure, and you realize what is most important to all parents: their children. It is time to return to the magic carpet and for you to return to your mother before she begins to worry about you. Let us be gone."

They hurried away from the dark mountains and returned to the beach where their carpet was awaiting. They quickly jumped on. Off into the beautiful blue sky they soared. Quick as a wink they were back home, and their mom was there to greet them. Ramor had taken them directly to their apartment on this trip, because they were running late, and he didn't want their mom to worry unnecessarily. Supper was waiting for them on the dinner table, and they rushed into the house to wash their hands.

Just as they sat down for dinner, Lisa said, "Mother, we have a beautiful surprise for you."

Lisa took out the diamond and gave it to her mother. Their mom was astounded at its beauty! And do you know what? That's the very diamond ring she wears on her hand to this day! A diamond from a pirate's treasure!

Ice and Snow

After their last adventure, the children were very tired and, upon clearing the dinner table, were ready for bed. It was late fall and of course it was getting dark very early in the evening. There was no time for playing outside after dinner. They put on their warmest pajamas and jumped into bed between the cold, cold sheets. That night, Lisa dreamed about getting all dressed up and going shopping with her mom; David dreamed about driving a red racing car; Stacy dreamed about playing with her Barbie dolls; and Karen dreamed of eating a great big dish of chocolate ice cream.

While everyone else was sleeping, Lisa began to stir and woke up just after midnight. She didn't know what it was that had awakened her, but she felt that something was not quite right. She decided to look out of the window to see if it were light yet. Upon doing so, she cried out, "Momma, David, Stacy, Karen, come quickly!"

When they got there, all Lisa could say was "Look!"

Everyone pressed their noses to the window and saw that the ground was covered with a blanket of white snow. The snow was coming down heavily. When they looked up at the streetlights, they saw the snow rapidly swirling. The older children hadn't seen snow for a long time, and it was the first time for Stacy and Karen. After a while, their breath began to fog up the window, and the glass began to get a little cold on their noses.

"OK, children," Mother said, "get ready for a special treat. I want everyone to run and get on their snowsuits, and we are going out to play in the snow—right now, in the middle of the night! People might think we are crazy, but we are going out to enjoy this snow. I'll get the sled and be right back."

It didn't take long for everyone to become wide awake. They got their heavy clothing on in a flash. Lisa put on her new red boots. They went out together, holding hands so that the little ones wouldn't fall on any ice that might be hidden beneath the snow. They could hear the squeak of the snow under their boots as they walked on the snowy ground. The snow was still coming down and felt cold as it blew against their faces.

They took turns riding their new sled down the hill in front of the apartments. Lisa rode with Karen, and David rode with Stacy. They fell off several times and had a tumble in the snow. The snow stuck to their clothes, and soon they began to look like little roly-poly snow-men. The children and their mom were the only ones outside in the neighborhood. They had the night and the snow all to themselves. The snow was fresh and white and made everything look like a fairy kingdom. It was a beautiful sight to behold.

Soon they talked their mom into making a snowman. Everyone began to roll the snow into three large snowballs: two snowballs for the body and a smaller snowball for the head. The consistency of the snow was just right for sticking together, and, before they knew it, a snowman stood before their eyes. He needed a nose, eyes, mouth, and clothing to make him look real.

"I'll go get an old hat and scarf out of the house," Mother said. "Your dad, I'm sure, won't mind if we let the snowman use his old pipe."

When they were through adding the accessories, they stepped back to admire their handiwork. Mom brought out her camera with the flashcubes and took a picture of the children gathered around their snowman. He was a magnificent snowman, probably one of the best snowmen that had ever been made.

"OK, kids," Mom said, "it's two o'clock in the morning, and we had better go inside before we wake up the entire neighborhood. I'm glad tomorrow is Saturday and you can sleep late. If I know you children, you will be up at the crack of dawn anyway and ready to go back outside to enjoy the snow and your snowman before he melts."

Everyone reluctantly came inside. They took off their wet clothing and shoes and left them on the hall floor. The warm apartment felt good. While everyone was getting into their pajamas, Mom fixed delicious hot chocolate for all to enjoy. It hit the spot with creamy, white marshmallows melted on top. Everyone was getting sleepy, and poor Karen fell asleep right in her chair. Mother gently carried her to her bed and kissed her goodnight. Then everyone else tip-toed to bed. Boy, did they sleep well the rest of the night! What a wonderful night of fun that had been!

As Mom predicted, everyone was up bright and early in the morning. The children had pancakes for breakfast and drank more hot chocolate to prepare themselves for the snow outside. They went out into the cold air and sunshine and were playing in a flash. They weren't gone for long before they ran back in the house shouting, "Momma, Momma, our snowman is melting."

Stacy wanted to know why their snowman was melting just when they were having such fun. "Well," Mom said, "we have to be thankful for our joys and pleasures when we have them. Just like many other things, some moments of pleasure are fleeting. There will always be more snow and more snowmen to build. Now you have something to look forward to in the future. You can use your vivid imagination and dream about that next snowman that you are going to build."

"Come on, everybody," David said, "let's go back out while we can still play in the snow."

Lisa added, "Why not go down to see Ramor and find out what kind of adventure he has in store for us?"

Off they went, hand in hand, down to their oak tree by the stream. The stream appeared to be frozen solid now, but the children knew not to walk on the ice, because it might not hold their weight. They had no trouble finding the old oak tree. The leaves had mostly fallen off, and now they could see mistletoe in the high branches of the tree. The mistletoe was green and leafy with little white berries (poisonous, so don't eat them). Mistletoe means "tree thief." It is a parasite that lives off the nutrients of the tree. A squirrel with an acorn in its mouth suddenly jumped into a hole in the tree, which must have been its nest for the winter.

"Well, here we are," said Lisa. "Let's call Ramor."

No sooner had she said his name than he was instantly there, with his long white beard and rosy cheeks. He, too, had his boots on, but they were black.

"Hello, my little friends," he said. "I'm glad to see you. I have a friend of yours here with me."

They looked around, and there was their snowman right beside him. My, were they surprised!

"Hello there, children," said the snowman. "I'm glad you have come, because Ramor and I want to take you to the land of ice and snow, so that you may visit my home."

The children couldn't believe that their snowman was talking, but then they remembered the magical powers of Ramor. They couldn't wait to get started on this new adventure. Just when they thought they had lost their snowman, there he was!

Top of the World

The children gathered around Ramor and the snowman. They were so excited about the thought of visiting the snowman's home. The snowman was anxious to get started, because he was beginning to become a little warm, and you know what happens when snow gets warm. It melts, and that could be disastrous for a snowman.

"OK, Lisa, you hold Karen's hand, and David, you hold Stacy's hand. We'll jump onto the magic carpet and take a ride," said Ramor.

The carpet was beside the oak tree, and Ramor had to push the accumulated snow off it before the children could get on. The snowman sat in the front so he could assist in guiding the carpet to his home. It had been quite some time since Ramor had visited there. It was getting a little dark, and high in the sky you could just barely see the stars. The snowman told Ramor that the best way to get to his house was to fly toward the North Star. The North Star hangs in the heavens right above the North Pole and is a very easy star on which to guide. It is easy to locate in the sky, because two stars on the lip of the Big Dipper constellation always point toward it.

It was a little chilly now, and the children were glad they had on their nice, warm coats. Lisa and David made sure that Stacy and Karen kept their mittens on and tucked their scarves in around their necks.

Soon the sun was completely down, and all around the children the stars looked like tiny lights hanging in the sky. Overhead, the stars clustered closely together and spread out into a cloudy band across the sky. This was called the "Milky Way." They were following along the Milky Way all the way to the North Pole, the "Top of the World."

David saw a shooting star and pointed it out to everyone.

Lisa said, "That will surely bring us good luck."

As they looked northward, they saw bright red and green lights rolling across the sky like a wave traveling through the ocean. It was here and there, and at times was even rather hazy looking.

"Isn't that just beautiful," Lisa exclaimed. "What is it, Ramor?"

"Those are called the Northern Lights," Ramor replied. "No one really knows what causes them, although some say they are caused by particles from the sun bouncing off the earth's atmosphere. They are beautiful, and, like many things in nature, even if we don't understand them, we can certainly enjoy and appreciate them."

The Northern Lights put on a spectacular show for the children to see. It was almost like the Fourth of July. Lisa and David could remember all the bright fireworks they had seen in celebrations when they lived in Hawaii, but Stacy and Karen were too young to remember, even though they had been born there.

"We are just about at the North Pole," said the snowman. "Start to slow the carpet down, Ramor."

It was a short night way up here by the North Pole, and already the sun was peeking up from over the horizon. This time of year it was mostly daylight at the North Pole, but in six months, the snow people would spend most of their time in darkness. Everything was white. The children had never seen so much ice and snow. There were tall mountains that looked like they were made entirely of snow. Every now and then they could see in the distance what appeared to be rivers running through the ice that led into the vast ocean. In many places the snow and ice looked bluish in color. The snowman told them that the reflection of the bright blue sky on the snow made it appear light blue in color. It was certainly a very beautiful sight! Everything looked so clean and fresh.

The air was cold now, and, when the children took in a deep breath, they could feel the cold air rushing into their lungs. They could see their breath as the warm air they breathed out was surrounded by the colder air outside and turned to mist. They came in for a landing and sat down right smack in the center of Snow City, North Pole.

All the snowmen and snow women (and snow boys and snow girls) rushed out to greet the snowman, Ramor, and the children. A great big snowman enthusiastically welcomed them to the North Pole (he must have been the mayor of Snow City) and invited them to visit his home; and by the way, his house was made completely of blocks of packed snow. Even though the house was made of snow, the air inside was warm enough for the children to take off their coats and mittens.

The snow mother said, "Children, I have a special treat for you so sit down and make yourselves comfortable while I bring you something to eat."

Of course, you guessed it: She brought them snow ice cream to eat, and it was covered with a special sauce. The children didn't leave a drop. It was so delicious, and they were very hungry from their long journey. They really weren't tired, because they were too excited to sleep and wanted to see everything that there was to see at the North Pole.

David asked the mayor if they were right at the tip-top of the world, and he replied, "Almost. Soon we will take a sled ride to the top of the world, so that you will have an amazing and special journey to remember all of your life. I know that you will be excited to tell your friends about this visit when you go back home."

They went outside the mayor's house, and it just amazed the children to see so many people made of snow. All of the snow people looked happy and kind and were always smiling. Everyone was polite and said hello or good morning when they passed the children.

"Now, children," Ramor said, "the mayor and I will ride on the carpet to the North Pole, but you can ride on these dog sleds. It is not too far, and the dogs know the way. We have two teams here. David, you will drive one sleigh, and Lisa, you will drive the other. Karen will ride with Lisa, and Stacy will ride with David. Each of you has seven dogs on your team. Lisa, your lead dog is called Snowflake, and David, your lead dog is called Snowball. Stacy and Karen, you get onto the sleighs and let us bundle you up in blankets, as this cold air is just freezing. All you have to do now is crack your whips and the dogs will take you."

"Crack!" went the whips and off they went. The two sleighs with the children were speeding their way across the vast openness toward the North Pole, the Top of the World.

Birthday Party

The race was on. The dogs were barking loudly as the two sleighs raced over the snow and ice toward the North Pole.

"Come on, Snowflake," Lisa urged. "Let's go!"

"Mush, Snowball, mush!" David said. (You say mush to husky dogs to make them go faster.)

On they went with the snow blowing in their faces and the wind blowing their hair. The two little sisters were bundled up, one in each sleigh, just laughing and having the best old time. As far around as everyone could see there was nothing but snow and ice. It was really a very beautiful site to behold. They saw only stark whiteness against the blue, blue sky.

Up ahead in the distance they could just barely make out two figures. It must have been Ramor and the mayor of Snow City. As they approached, the figures became larger and larger until the children could definitely see that it was their two friends. As they pulled their sleighs right across the Top of the World, the North Pole, wouldn't you guess, the big race ended in a tie.

David, however, being a little gentleman said, "Lisa, I'm sure that you just barely beat me."

They laughed and got out of their sleighs to look around. All four children could hardly believe that they were standing on the Top of the World. Nearby was a little hut where they could shelter themselves from the cold, and so, in they went. Inside there was a sign that read, "You are now on Top of the World. Take the pen attached to this placard and sign your name in the book below so all who come here will know that you, too, have made this fantastic journey to the Top of the World." Lisa and David signed their names, and Lisa signed for Stacy and Karen.

Just then they saw something white moving outside the hut, and the children rushed out to see what had passed by. They saw Ramor and the mayor talking to, of all things, a large polar bear.

"Come over here, children," Ramor said, "and you can have a ride on the polar bear's back."

He was a big bear, and to little Karen and Stacy he looked as big as an elephant. All four of the children were able to get on his back at the same time. They held on to his soft, white fur and were very comfortable, as the polar bear loped around with them on his back. There was a large hole in the ice, so the polar bear jumped in while being very careful not to get the children wet. He swam around for a while with the children just laughing and having the best old time on his back. It isn't every day that you get to ride on a real polar bear's back. The polar bear soon got out of the water and took the children over to Ramor. He knelt down so that the children could slide off of his back. It was just like going down a slick, wet sliding board!

Then Ramor said, "Come over here, children. I want to show you something else."

And right there behind a large mound of snow was a whole family of penguins. Now Lisa and David knew that there were only penguins at the South Pole. They had read that in a *National Geographic* magazine for kids, and wondered how all of these cute little penguins happened to be here at the North Pole. Ramor told her that many thousands of years ago all of the penguins except a few were stranded on a big ice flow and floated all the way to the South Pole. These penguins were the last descendants of those

fewthat were left at the North Pole. These were the very last penguins at the North Pole, and they were something special.

Some of the penguins were as tall as Karen and Stacy. The penguins strutted around following one another and slipping and sliding over the ice into a pool of water. They seemed to be having a great time. A baby penguin came over to the children, and they were able to pet it and feel its soft feathers. All of the penguins looked like they had on black jackets with white shirts, but of course that was just the color of their feathers.

"Now you are in for a real treat," Ramor said. "It is time to go back to Snow City for a big surprise." They then left for Snow City on the magic carpet. (The mayor would get the sled dogs later on.) They landed in the middle of town, and this time no one was around to greet them. The children wondered where everyone had gone.

The mayor said, "Follow me, everyone."

He led them to a large building, made of snow blocks, and they went inside. No sooner had they entered than they heard a loud, "Surprise!" They looked around and saw hundreds of the snow people gathered around smiling at them, and all started to sing "Happy birthday to you." It was a surprise birthday party!

The mayor came up and said, "This party is to celebrate your recent birthdays, Stacy and David, and also for Karen, since hers is next month. It will also be for Lisa, since she won't be here when hers comes around in June. We can all celebrate together."

They brought in a tremendous birthday cake that was taller than Stacy and had so many candles on it that it was shining like a star. The children made a wish and blew out all of the candles on the cake with the help of Ramor's magic. Lisa cut the cake, and David and the younger sisters helped pass plates of it around. It was delicious and like no other cake they had ever eaten. It was so good that all of the children had at least two pieces (David ate three). Finally, when the cake was gone, a small snow girl brought out gifts for Lisa, Stacy, and Karen, and a little snow boy brought out a gift for

David. They excitedly opened their presents. Stacy and Karen got little wind-up penguin dolls. Lisa got a stuffed toy polar bear to put on her bed, and David got a ball. It was a very special kind of snowball that could bounce and could be played with like a regular ball and was different from any other snowball. Ramor told David that this one would never melt!

David just then happened to look at his watch and reminded Ramor that it was getting late, and perhaps they should be on their way home.

Lisa said, "Let me get a picture of everyone with my new camera before we go." (That girl just carries her camera everywhere.)

After that, they said farewell to all the snow people and began their long journey home, where they knew that their mom would be waiting with a nice, hot meal. Once again they arrived just in time for supper. No one ate very much that night, and Mother guessed why after they told her about the delicious birthday cake they had just eaten at the North Pole.

"You children have such marvelous adventures," Mother said. "I wonder where you will be going next."

Ants and Other Little Things

The weather had turned unseasonably warm for wintertime. It was Saturday afternoon; the young children were up from their naps, and everyone was outside playing. Lisa thought of a great game to play. She said, "Let's lie on our backs on the grass and look up at the sky. Each person will get a chance to tell what kind of shapes he sees in the puffy, white clouds above us."

They found a nice dry spot on the grass and lay down side by side, looking into the sky, being sure not to look at the sun. The bright sun was warm and really felt good, as there was still a little chill in the air.

David spoke up first. "That one looks just like Popeye's face! One little cloud even looks like a sailor's cap on top of his head."

"That's very good," replied Lisa. "Look over there. That one is shaped just like a map of the United States."

Stacy spoke up next and said, "That one looks just like our cousin's dog, Snoopy. I just can't wait for us to get a little dog."

Karen pointed to some clouds and said, "Flowers." Sure enough a group of small clouds looked like a bouquet of flowers.

After a while the children rolled over and lay there talking to each other with their chins resting on the backs of their hands. Everyone was just sort of looking down into the grass. They could see the blades of grass, so green and sharp looking. Amongst the grass they could see the soil in the ground and all the little grains that went to make it up. Every now and then a little ant would haphazardly meander by.

"Lisa, don't you wish that we could make ourselves very small and walk among the blades of grass?" asked David. "I'll bet that those tiny grains of sand would look just like large boulders."

Lisa replied, "It would be like walking through a jungle. I wonder how the ants find their way. They always look like they are just wandering aimlessly around."

With the warm sun shining on them and everyone having had a big lunch, naturally all the children were a little sleepy. So they fell fast asleep there on the grass and, of course, just by chance, all had the same dream. (Perhaps Ramor had something to do with that.) The four children suddenly found themselves in rather a strange situation. You guessed it: They had all grown very small and, instead of looking down at the grass, were looking up through it. Deep in the grass like that, it was shady and cool. The blades of grass blocked much of the sunlight. Up this close, the grass looked very green and shiny, but one had to be very careful, as it was rather sharp along the edges. David was right. The grains of sand were now very large and made walking around very difficult.

Soon the children saw what looked like a monster coming, but they recognized it as an ant. It was a red ant with a large head and six legs. As it came closer, it stopped and looked at the children. It was as big as little Karen. It asked them who they were and where they came from and noted that they were unusual-looking ants themselves. Lisa immediately informed him that they were not ants.

The ant replied, "You're lucky you're not an ant. We work all the time and never have any fun."

Lisa replied, "Everyone should work hard but should also have fun and play too."

The ant said that, right now, they were busily preparing for the winter and carefully building up their anthills so everyone could stay inside and keep warm. They were also storing up their supply of food. "Why don't you come along with me and my friends," he said, "and we'll take you to our ant colony and show you how we live?"

Lisa responded, "I guess it will be all right, but how will we get there?"

The ant replied that he and his friends would give them a ride on their backs, because ants are very strong creatures and can lift many times their own weight. They each climbed onto a different red ant, and off they went at a slow pace, winding their way among the blades of grass. The children soon realized why the ants walk around so crazily. They were just trying to find the best place to walk to get home and many times had to take detours around the larger grains of dirt and sand that blocked their paths.

All of a sudden the ant in the lead with David on his back called out excitedly, "We'd better hurry. I thought I saw some black ants coming from behind that weed patch."

Now at that time the red ants and the black ants did not get along too well, so the red ants, being rather small little fellows, decided that they had better get out of there in a hurry. The children had to hold on tight as the ants started to run toward their home. The red ants were hoping that the black ants wouldn't see them, and that they would get back to their colony before being noticed. Their anthill wasn't too far ahead, but the black ants were coming their way fast. What was going to happen? What should they do?

Ants Can Be Friends

The black ants weren't too far behind the red ants, as they raced around clumps of grass, tall weeds, and grains of sand that were as big as boulders. The children were having a good time riding on the ants' backs, but it really was rather bumpy and difficult to stay on. Up ahead they soon saw the red mound of sand, which ants always build around the entrance to their tunnels into the ground. There was a path up the side of the sandy slope, and up it the red ants quickly ran into the safety of their home. The children had to duck their heads to fit into the entrance, but once inside the ground there was plenty of room, even for standing up. The inside of the tunnel was smooth. The ants had done much work pulling out the roots that hung down to block the way.

One ant said, "We will take you to the queen. She will be very happy to meet you."

The children were excited to meet a queen, even if she was only an ant. As ants go, the queen was rather pretty and welcomed them graciously into her home. She asked if they would like something to eat, and they all replied, "Yes, please."

There was a table on one side of the throne room that had large white crystals on it, which looked like diamonds, only much larger. The queen said that they were granules of sugar and invited the children to taste them. (Ants just love sugar.) It tasted very good, but was so sweet that the children just couldn't eat very much of it. The sugar was very filling, though, and gave them lots of energy.

Lisa said, "Miss Queen, we are all very thirsty. Do you have any water we could drink?"

The queen pointed to an underground spring of fresh water in the distant part of the chamber. The children went over to it. Of course ants don't use cups, so the children had to scoop the water out of the little stream using their hands. After they had had enough to drink, David asked the queen why the black ants were chasing them.

The queen, who wore a crown of tiny flowers on her head, answered, "For years the black ants have wanted to live here close to the path to the grocery store. We have a wonderful location, because people who go to and from the store often drop food, or sometimes there might be a hole in a bag of sugar, and often in just a few weeks we can gather enough food to last us all winter. We have plenty of fresh water, and the big trees shelter us from the rain and snow. In the summer there are many flowers growing nearby for us to decorate our homes. As you can see, I just love fresh flowers." The children had already noticed the crown of flowers on her head.

Lisa then said, "Well, isn't there plenty of food and room for both you and the black ants to live here?"

The queen replied, "Yes, but every time we talk with each other, it ends up in an argument, and we go back to fighting."

Lisa said, "I'll talk to them for you, Miss Queen, and we'll see what we shall see."

In the meantime, the black ants were waiting outside. They were too big to fit down the red ants' tunnel. Lisa walked out of the tunnel, and when she walked down the mound of sand (the ant hill), a black ant came up to her. Again, they wanted to know what kind of ant she was, and she assured them that she was not an ant but was a little girl. (David stayed inside the anthill with Stacy and Karen, because they wanted to play with the ant babies.)

Lisa immediately said to the black ants, "Why are you chasing the red ants and bullying them around? You know that isn't a very nice thing to do."

The leader of the black ants, their queen replied, "We lived here years ago and still feel that this is our homeland, and we have decided to move back. The land where we live now has had a famine, and there is very little food for us there. The red ants have moved here, but we want to come back."

Lisa said, "Don't you realize that the red ants want to be your friends? They would love to have you here as their neighbors. There is plenty of food for all and as much room as you need for your own anthills. You have been so busy fighting with the red ants that you really haven't taken the time to listen to what they have been trying to tell you."

The black ant queen was embarrassed. She had been so busy chasing the red ants around that she had forgotten that arguments could also be settled in a friendly way. She realized that the whole kingdom (the kingdom of the black ants and the kingdom of the red ants) could settle their differences the same way a single person (or ant) could settle his differences with another individual.

The black ant queen then said, "Lisa, please ask the red ant queen to come out to see me."

Lisa was happy. She knew that her efforts would bring peace and happiness to all ants everywhere. The red ant queen came out of the anthill and approached the black ant queen. She gave the ant sign of friendship by crossing her two front legs. The black ant queen did likewise, and this indicated to all that from now on red ants and black ants would live in friendship. The black ants immediately got busy building their anthill right next door to the red ants. The red ants brought over some of their sugar crystals to share with the black ants, and they all got along just fine. Stacy and Karen helped carry the sugar over to the black ants' new dwelling. David and Lisa were busily helping the black ants build their anthill and were carrying the grains of sand out from where the ants were tunneling into the ground. Everyone was so happy to be able to get along.

Lisa decided that it was time for them to return home but was worried, since she didn't know how to get there. Ramor wasn't with them on this trip. "Oh my, what will we do now?" she thought.

Just then she looked around and saw the other three children lying down in the grass, but they didn't seem to be small any more. She stood up and said, "It all must have been a dream."

She woke the other sleeping children, and they said at once, "Lisa, guess what I dreamed."

"I know," she replied. "We all had the same dream. Even though Ramor wasn't here, he was looking out for us. I'll bet he saw to it that we had this adventure with the ants. We had better go inside. The sun is starting to set, and it's turning cold again. Let's hurry and tell our mom what happened."

They ran into the house and excitedly told their mom about their latest adventure.

And do you know that to this very day the ants are special friends of the four little children, Lisa, David, Stacy, and Karen. They would never think of stepping on an ant! Every time an ant sees one of them, it waves. The ants are happy that the four little children showed them that ants could be friends, no matter whether they are red or black.

Aloha

"Aloha," Lisa said.

Stacy looked around at Lisa and asked, "What's that mean, Lisa?" They had been playing dolls in Lisa's room.

Lisa was about to leave and said, "*Aloha* means both 'hello' and 'good-bye' in Hawaiian. You ought to know, Stacy. You and Karen were born there."

"I know," Stacy answered, "I wanna go back and maybe Ramor can take us."

Lisa replied, "That's a pretty good idea. Perhaps we could ask Ramor to take us there on his magic carpet for an afternoon. I'll bet that David and Karen would enjoy the trip, too. Let's find them. Put up your dolls and come with me, Stacy."

Lisa and Stacy went outside to find David and Karen, who were playing on the swings. Lisa and Stacy told them their idea about going to Hawaii, and both David and Karen thought it would be great fun. David reminded everyone to wear a bathing suit under their clothes so they could go swimming in the ocean and perhaps even jump some waves.

Lisa said that it was too late for them to go that day, but just by luck, there was a teachers' meeting at school the next day, and all the classes were getting out early. She and David would hurry home from school, and they could go in search of Ramor and hopefully start on a new adventure.

The next day, right on schedule, Lisa and David came home at 11:30 AM. Their little sisters had taken an early nap and were up for lunch with the big children. They had hot vegetable soup and grilled cheese sandwiches with potato chips and pickles on the side. The hot soup hit the spot, as the weather was clear but very cold.

Mother wondered why they rushed around looking for their bathing suits when they all finished lunch. "Now wait a minute," she said. "Just what is going on around here?"

Karen replied, "We're goin' to why-ee!"

All Mother could say was, "Oh, my, I guess that you and your friend Ramor are going on another adventure. Well, let me help you find your swimming suits before you children have all the clothes on the floor."

It didn't take long for Mom to find a swimming suit for each child. They put them on under their clothing and went outside to look for Ramor so he could take them on a new adventure to Hawaii.

"Ramor! Ramor! Ramor!" they all shouted when they came upon their special oak tree. In a flash he was there, because when his friends called, he always came immediately.

"Hello, little children. It's good to see you again. Did you have fun with the ants on your last adventure? You thought that I wasn't there, but I was watching you all the time. Now, how about a little trip to Hawaii this time? What do you say?"

The children were astounded that Ramor knew what they had been planning. "Let's get going right away," Ramor said, "as it is so cold here and so nice and warm and sunny in Hawaii. Everyone climb onto the magic carpet, and off we will go."

This time the carpet took off like a flash, heading west and into the sun. They traveled so fast that the sun didn't seem to move at all in the sky. It was almost as if time were standing still. They crossed the

Mississippi River, the flatlands of Texas and Oklahoma, until finally they could see the Painted Desert up ahead. It was glistening in the sunlight with all the colors of the rainbow. Then they saw the breathtaking Grand Canyon, then Lake Tahoe, and in no time they were hovering over Los Angeles.

"Look down there," said David, "it's the San Diego Freeway. That was some visit we had to the San Diego Zoo last June. Hey everyone, look back there. I can see the Matterhorn at Disneyland."

By that time they were departing over the ocean. All they could see for miles and miles ahead was water, water, and more water. Karen and Stacy began to wonder how much farther they had to go. Ramor told them that the distance from Los Angeles to Hawaii was 2,200 miles. As fast as they were going, though, it surely wouldn't take much time. Just then, David spotted a big white ship below them, and he said it looked just like the Matson Lines luxury ocean liner, the *Lurline*. The children remembered what a good time they had had on the *Lurline* on their trip from Hawaii to California when they moved back to the mainland.

Suddenly, up ahead the children saw a large mountain rising into the clouds on the Big Island, Hawaii. They saw clouds of smoke, too, and thought perhaps there might have been a volcanic eruption in the Kilauea crater located there. They asked Ramor to take the carpet down toward the mountain and fly over the fire pit so they could watch the flames leaping high into the air and see the molten lava flowing inside the crater. The closer they came, the more beautiful the mountain looked, rising straight up out of the water into the sky. Soon they were over the crater and could see the fire and smoke leaping high into the air. The children were amazed at what they saw and decided they didn't want to get any closer to the fire pit. They would be excited to tell all their friends about seeing the inside of a live volcano. It was quite an experience. The air above the volcano was hot and dry and smelled strongly of sulfur, which smells just like rotten eggs!

The blue-green water up ahead looked beautiful, as they continued traveling toward the island of Oahu. Lisa suggested they stop in the pineapple fields to enjoy fresh pineapple, and later they could take a refreshing swim in the ocean. Ramor landed the carpet on a barren spot in the middle of one of the pineapple fields, and the children got off the carpet and stretched their legs. In a minute Ramor was with them, holding two large juicy pineapples. He had sliced them neatly and passed the luscious fruit around for all to enjoy. It was so good and sweet that each of them had seconds.

David suggested they go over to Kailua Beach on the windward side of the island for their swim. It was not too far from where they used to live in Kaneohe. They got back onto the carpet and, in a split second, were landing in a large, expansive, grassy area behind Kailua Beach. Surprisingly, they were the only ones at the beach that afternoon. Most people were in town watching a special Aloha Day parade. They pulled off their top clothing, having had their bathing suits on underneath, and held hands while running over the beach to the water. They were ready to have some real fun at the ocean!

Water Wonderland

The children were amazed to see the big waves splashing onto the shore. They waded into the surf letting the water roll in and out around their legs and feet. As the water rolled back into the sea, the sand under their feet would wash away, making them feel as though they, too, were sliding into the ocean along with the salt water. Karen and Stacy held hands and sat down in the shallow water to play, while Lisa and David moved out a little deeper to jump the waves. They would watchfully wait, and, when a big wave came, they would jump high in the water and let the wave gently pass around them with the salt water splashing up into their little noses. It was so much fun having the water support them as they gradually floated back toward shore.

Every now and then, Lisa and David would glance back at the shoreline to make sure that the little children were doing OK. Karen and Stacy were having so much fun playing on the beach. They had found two small buckets and shovels and were digging in the sand. They would fill their buckets, tamp the damp sand down, and then turn the bucket upside down onto the beach. The sand would come out in the shape of the inside of the bucket. They had dumped over two bucketfuls, but the sand was wet and made the bucket very difficult for them to handle. They called to Lisa and David to come help them.

Lisa said, "Come on, David; let's go help the babies make a drip castle in the sand. I'll bet they've never made one before."

The big children hurried back to the shore. They both swam in on a big wave and let it carry them to the shoreline. The little girls were happy for them to help, and everyone got busy making the castle. They dug a hole in the sand above the waterline and poured water into it so they would have nice, moist sand to drip down their finger-tips to form a myriad of shapes to make up their castle. Everyone was having the best time imaginable.

After a while, Ramor came onto the beach to see how everyone was getting along. He knew they would soon be getting hungry so he brought along a basket of food. Everyone thought that it would be best to spread out their lunch on the grass rather than on the sandy beach. They found a shady spot under a coconut palm tree and proceeded to have their lunch. There were several coconuts lying on the ground at the base of the palm tree, and while Lisa was setting up their picnic, the two little sisters played with the coconuts, rolling them around like beach balls. Ramor had brought lemonade and sandwiches made with a special kind of spread that was abso-lutely delicious. For dessert, they cut a freshly baked chocolate cake that Ramor had just picked up from Tiki Tops bakery in the nearby village of Kaneohe. Everything was delicious, and the chil-dren enjoyed every mouthful of their lunch!

After lunch they decided to take a walk down the beach, since they knew not to go swimming right after eating, because they might get a cramp. As they walked, they looked out at the colorful sailboats skimming over the water and bounding through the waves. White seagulls were flying overhead and made a pretty pic-ture against the blue sky. They enjoyed seeing the rows of swaying palm trees with coconuts in them lined up along the beachfront. They walked and talked and occasionally ran along the shoreline.

Soon they spotted a small island not too far out in the water and wondered what might be found on it. They thought it would be fun to take a sail on one of the boats and explore the little island. Of course, Ramor took care of that. Suddenly, in front of them there appeared a red boat with blue and white sails. All they needed to do now was to get in and push off into the water. Ramor said he was a special friend of the good west wind, and that his friend would blow the boat straight to the little island.

The four children hopped into the boat and put on life vests. The wind filled the sails and blew them across the shallow water and out into the great ocean. It was a pleasant ride, and the children enjoyed the wind in their faces and the salt water splashing on them from over the side of the boat. They were in their bathing suits and didn't mind getting a little wet. Ramor was at the tiller, safely steering the boat. In a short while the boat gently glided to a halt on the sandy beach of the pretty little island.

When they got off, the first thing that Lisa spotted was a large plumeria tree filled with white blossoms tinged with yellow. The flowers had a wonderfully sweet smell. Lisa told Stacy and Karen about making leis for special occasions with the plumeria flowers when they had lived in Hawaii. The trees had been growing right in their own backyard. The little island also had a sandy beach, but this beach, unlike the beach on shore, had beautiful seashells all over it. The children ran up and down the beach collecting pretty shells to take home to show their mom. Ramor had brought a laundry bag to hold the seashells once they had been collected.

After a while, they were tired out from picking up the pretty shells and sat down on the beach in the shallow water to rest. Ramor sat with them and softly said, "Did you children know that there is a beautiful water world underneath the waves? I'm going to take you beneath the sea and show you all the fish and perhaps even a mermaid or two. Of course, I'll have to do a little magic so you will be able to breathe and swim for a long time under water, but that will be no problem."

He then said a few strange words, looked up at the children, and with a wave of his hand motioned for them to follow him into the "Water Wonderland."

Under the Sea

The children were excited with the anticipation of actually going under the sea and swimming around like a fish. They were a little worried as to how they would manage to breathe under water but had confidence that good old Ramor would take care of them. It was a nice feeling to know that they always had Ramor to trust and look after them. After Ramor had said his special words, the children felt a strange urge to go into the water. They held hands and followed Ramor into the sea. Before long, the water was right up to Stacy and Karen's little noses. They then just dived into the next wave, and lo and behold, they could swim as well as the fish and could breathe under the water as well. It was a very strange sensation.

It was a bright and sunny day, and the light made the bottom of the ocean shimmer like it was covered with diamonds and silver. The coral was a beautiful pink color, but they knew to be careful near the reef, as it was sharp enough to scrape and cut. They saw hundreds of tiny fish swimming in schools, darting in and out of the coral. The ocean floor was covered with seashells and sand dollars and had seaweed growing that was taller than Lisa. The seaweed swayed in the current and took on all sorts of shapes as it moved to and fro in the water. Lisa and David remembered how the aquarium looked at Sea Life Park and felt as though they were swimming around right inside it. They saw big fish, little fish, flat fish, skinny fish, happy-looking fish, and sad-looking fish; some of them even had faces that looked like people.

Soon they came upon a group of dolphins. Actually, these were porpoises and looked very much like Flipper. Now, porpoises are very smart mammals, as the older children well knew. There were five of them, and they were playing a game of tag in the water. They were swimming around so fast that it made the children dizzy just to watch them.

Ramor said, "Come on, children. I want each of you to take hold of a porpoise's tail, and they will take you to the underwater city."

Each of the children took hold of a porpoise's tail, and off they went. The porpoises swam so fast that the children felt as though they were flying through the water. Their feet were straight out behind them, and it was all that they could do to hang on. The porpoises would occasionally look back to make sure they didn't lose their passengers.

Soon they came to a city under the sea. The city was made of coral, and the people who lived there were not really people but were mermaids and mermen. These were beautiful women and men who had the upper body of a human and the tail of a fish. They ran the underwater city. Several of them cautiously came to greet the children. They wanted to show them around their underwater city. They first took the children to the fields where they grew their food. There were all sorts of strange vegetables growing; some looked like plain seaweed, but others looked like beans, peas, and other vegetables that they had eaten at home. Soon they came upon a grove of very short trees that had fruit on them about the size of apples, but they weren't apples, but more like berries. One of the mermaids said these were seaberry trees, and the fruit was very sweet and nutritious. Everyone ate seaberries under the ocean instead of meat.

In some of the other fields, dolphins were pulling plows, tilling the soil, while other smaller fish followed along behind dropping seeds into the ocean floor. Another group of sunfish came along last and covered the seeds with the sandy soil by flapping their fins vigorously. It caused the water to get very cloudy, but when it cleared, the sandy soil settled, and the seeds were all covered up.

David wanted to know if any sharks lived down there with them, and the mermaid answered with a shrill whistle. In a flash, the largest shark they had ever seen swam up to them. It was really fierce looking and had very large teeth.

"Down here," the mermaid said, "everyone lives in friendship. Sharks aren't really too bad, but they do have very short tempers. They stay pretty much to themselves, but old Sharky here is all right and is a good friend. He has a very tender nose, so be sure that you don't bump it." The big shark didn't stay long and soon swam away.

As they walked farther, things quickly got very dark. The children thought it was suddenly nighttime, but in the distance they could still see daylight. They wondered what had happened. What was blocking out the light?

The mermaid said, "Well look who came to see you! It's good old Elmer, the blue whale, the largest of mammals. He is so big that he blocks out the light. Elmer really likes children. He used to swim at Sea Life Park Aquarium and put on shows for all the people, but he became so lonesome that they sent him back home to the sea."

Elmer was so big and long that they could see his face but not his tail. He looked like he was smiling, and it was funny to see a whale grin. The mermaid said that Elmer would let the children stand right inside of his mouth. He opened his mouth very wide, and each of the children grabbed hold of one of his big teeth and pulled themselves right up into his mouth. Lisa said she wished she had brought her camera to take a picture of this. David said he couldn't wait to tell the other children in school about standing in a whale's mouth.

Just then Ramor looked at his watch and said, "We had better move along. Your mom will begin to worry where you children are. We've been gone for quite a long time. Grab hold of your porpoises, and we will head on back to shore."

In a flash, the porpoises carried them back to the beach. The children stood there waving as the porpoises dived back into the deep sea. It wasn't too much longer before the children were back at the old oak tree and changed into dry clothing. Stacy and Karen clapped their hands with delight over the trip and Karen kept saying, "Wanna go back, wanna see why-ee!"

Before the children left the underwater city, a mermaid had given each of them seaberry seeds to plant when they got home. They would wait until the warm spring and plant their seeds outside their windows. They couldn't wait to tell their mom where they had been. They would give her the seeds to put away until it was time to plant them in the spring. They would be the only children in the world to have a crop of wonderfully delicious and nutritious seaberries.

When Mom saw them she said, "You children certainly have beautiful suntans. Where did Ramor take you on this trip?"

Lisa said, "Mom, you just won't believe it, but we'll tell you anyway."

At the end of Lisa's account of their adventure, Mom said, "That's absolutely fantastic, but now it's time for you little fish to get into bed."

By this time the younger girls were so exhausted that they had fallen asleep right there on the living room floor.

"Good night, Lisa, David, Stacy, and Karen. I love you!" said Mom. "Get plenty of rest. Who knows where your friend Ramor will take you on your next adventure."

Dogs

It was another dreary Saturday morning. The sky was gray and over-cast, and there was a slight drizzle coming down. The weather had been cold, but things had warmed up a bit with the rain. Everything was still quiet in the household. Stacy and Karen were both sleeping. Lisa and David were watching cartoons in the den, and Mom was having a cup of coffee while she read last night's paper.

Just then, two little noses peeked around the corner of the living room, and two little voices said, "We're up." It was Karen and Stacy.

Everyone kissed them good morning, and the toddlers came into the den to also watch cartoons. Mom announced that she was going into the kitchen to fix a special Saturday morning breakfast—blueberry pancakes. Everyone licked their lips with the anticipation of such good things to eat. Soon breakfast was over, and the kitchen had been cleaned.

All the children went into Lisa's room to play school for a while. Lisa was the teacher; Karen was her helper; Stacy was saying her ABCs; and David was practicing his writing. Everyone was enjoying themselves, but soon they felt like doing something different. They wandered over to the window beside Lisa's bed and stared out at the pouring rain. It was really coming down now.

David looked at Lisa and said, "Say, Lisa, what does it mean when they say, 'It's raining cats and dogs?'"

Lisa replied, "I guess all they mean is that it is raining very, very hard. I've heard people say that before, and I guess that's all it means."

"I sure will be glad when we get a dog," said David. "It will be fun to take care of it and to teach it dog tricks."

They all agreed to that.

Lisa said, "I wonder what the poor dogs do that are caught out on rainy days like this and don't have a home. Dogs do seem to have a lot of fun roaming around all day and playing. I bet they even sometimes stay out all night. It must be fun to be a dog. I wonder what it would be like."

"What kind of a dog would you like to be, Lisa?" asked David.

She replied, "Oh, I think that it would be fun to be a pretty little West Highland terrier named Frosty. David, I know that you'd want to be: a black Labrador retriever."

David asked, "What do you think that Karen and Stacy would want to be?"

"Let's see," responded Lisa. "Perhaps they would like to be two little cute cocker spaniels called Trixie and Dixie. How about you, David? We'd call you King. OK?"

The children were excited with all the talk about dogs. They noticed that the rain was beginning to slack off, but it was still a little cloudy outside.

David said, "Let's get on our raincoats and go find Ramor. Maybe he can find something exciting for us to do today."

Mother bundled all four children in their raincoats and rain boots and told them not to be gone too long, because it looked like it might start pouring again. The children assured her they would hurry back home if it started to rain again. With that, they kissed her good-bye and started out to look for Ramor.

The path down to their oak tree was a little muddy so they had to be careful not to get their boots all messed up. They hopped over and around the puddles and were just so happy to get outside once again. As they looked back over their shoulders, they could see a beautiful rainbow and felt that they had seen the last of the rain for a while. Everything was wet and shiny. The bushes and trees looked green and fresh, and the air smelled nice and clean. There was their old oak tree up ahead, towering above all the other trees around it. In a flash, there was their friend Ramor smiling down at them while sitting on one of the lower branches. He waved, and they waved back. He was happy to see them again.

"I know all about it," Ramor began. "You children are looking for something to do, and I've got just the thing. I happened to overhear your conversation in Lisa's bedroom about dogs. You had a lot of questions, and the best way to find the answer is to be a dog yourself. What do you think about that idea? Of course, you could change back into little children whenever you wanted to. All you would have to do is chase your tail and bark three times, and then you'd be yourselves once again. Do you want to give it a try? At least you would find out what it's like to be a dog."

"It sounds good to me," said David. Lisa nodded her head approvingly.

Karen and Stacy weren't quite so sure, but if Lisa and David thought it would be OK, then it would be just fine with them. Anyway, they thought that it would be fun to be a puppy, if only for a little while.

Ramor said, "I know what kind of dogs you want to be, so now all you have to do is close your eyes, and when you open them, I'll be gone, but you'll be dogs—and cute ones at that."

Lisa said, "OK, everyone, when I count to three, close your eyes— one, two, three."

They closed their eyes, and all of them began to feel rather strange. In just a minute they knew that there would be four dogs standing there instead of four little children.

"Open," Lisa said.

When they opened their eyes, they began to laugh. They were all dogs, and seeing dogs laugh is really a funny sight anyway. They were unique dogs, because they could still talk but could also bark. Karen had a funny bark that was rather squeaky. Lisa and Stacy had nice, ladylike barks, and David had rather a deep bark that scared everyone (even himself) at first.

There they were: David was a great big black Labrador retriever; Lisa was a snow-white West Highland terrier with a red bow on her head and a tail that waved in the air like a flag; and Stacy and Karen were two golden cocker spaniel puppies with long floppy ears.

"My, don't we all look funny!" exclaimed David.

"Well," Lisa said, "I guess we are funny-looking children, but mighty fine-looking dogs."

They pranced around looking at one another. "Let's find something to do," said David, and off they went, scampering down the path.

The pups (Stacy and Karen) had to run to keep up with the big dogs (David and Lisa). Off they went to see what a dog's world was like.

Doggone Fun

Off they went. Lisa, David, Stacy, and Karen ran as fast as their four doggy legs could carry them down the path.

"Come on, Stacy and Karen," David barked. "Let's hurry so we can scout around and meet some other dogs."

They were having a wonderful time running, since they could run so much faster with four legs than two. David, with his big, long, black Labrador legs, could run the fastest of all, but he and Lisa waited for the babies (I mean "pups") to catch up with them. They headed on down the path through the woods and stopped once to chase some pigeons that were eating seeds off the ground. You should have seen those birds scatter. All you could hear was the flapping of wings. After a while they ended up at the park and saw several other dogs playing around.

All four children (there I go again, I mean "dogs") climbed up the sliding board steps and came sliding down, standing on all fours. It was a funny sight to see four cute dogs sliding down the sliding board, but no one ever suspected that they were really four little children. Soon several of the other dogs gathered around and wondered where these four new dogs came from. Lisa answered that they all lived in the apartments around the corner. One beagle said that he knew where some good bones were buried, but the children told him that they would rather go home to eat, because they knew that they would have something good there waiting for them. The little beagle said he had been lost from his master (a little ten-year-old boy named Bryan). He told them that he, too, lived in the apartments but didn't know how to get home. The children (dogs) told the little beagle named Spunky to stay with them, and later on they would show him the way home. He was really happy. He had been very lonely and hadn't been getting enough to eat.

All the dogs (Lisa, David, Stacy, Karen, and Spunky) decided they would run up to the school and play in the schoolyard for a while. They stayed together and looked out for the pups as they crossed the street. It was Saturday afternoon, and no one else was in the schoolyard. Lisa and David wanted to show Karen, Stacy, and Spunky where their rooms were. After that they had to wait a minute while David scratched a flea that was biting him behind the ear. He thought that when he got his own dog he would keep a flea collar on his dog so the fleas wouldn't bother him.

Two other dogs wandered over and began to bother the girls, but then David (our big black Labrador) came over, and the two bothersome dogs ran off with their tails between their legs. Suddenly, Lisa said she smelled smoke. All the dogs ran over to see where it was coming from. They spotted flames in one of the basement rooms of the school and knew immediately that they had to get help to save their school from burning. All five dogs rushed to the house next door to the school and started barking as loudly as they could. In a few minutes, a nice lady came onto the front porch, and all the dogs ran up to her. She sensed that they wanted her to follow them, and off they went back to the school. The lady also saw the smoke and flames coming from the school and rushed back to her house to call the fire department. It didn't take long before three large, red, fire trucks with sirens screaming raced up to the schoolyard. In a short time, they connected their long hoses to the nearest fire hydrant and put out the fire with a steady stream of water. The lady told the fire chief, "You know, if it weren't for those five dogs over there, the school would have burned to the ground. They saved the school!"

The four children (dogs) said to Spunky, "It's time for us to run home now. We'll take you back to your house."

When they arrived at the apartments, Spunky knew exactly where to go to find his home and decided that he wouldn't wander off again. It was just too easy to get lost.

The four dogs then ran around in a circle chasing their tails and barked three times. They immediately changed back into children. When they got inside their apartment, all they could say was that they were doggone tired. They ate dinner and went to bed early that night.

Mom was reading the Sunday newspaper the next morning and said to the children, "Look at this article in the paper. It reads: 'Five dogs save school from burning down. The whole community is proud of these fine dogs for saving the school.'"

The children looked at one another and winked. They knew exactly who had saved the school from burning.

After breakfast, they told their mother that they were going out to play in the neighborhood with a new dog named Spunky.

Mother asked, "How in the world did you know about Spunky? I was talking to his owners just last night, and they said he was lost. They were very upset."

"He's back now," David said. Then they smiled and went on their way.

That was quite an unforgettable adventure! To this very day, no one knows that it was really the four little children who saved their school from burning down.

Campout

"We sure have been having wonderful adventures with our friend, Ramor," said Lisa.

"It's hard to believe we have done all the marvelous things that we have done," David added.

"Karen and me had a good time, too," said Stacy.

David scratched his head and said, "What do you think we ought to do today? The weather is nice, and it doesn't look like rain. Maybe Ramor will take us on a campout in the mountains. Let's see if it's OK with Mom if we stay out overnight. No telling where Ramor will want to take us."

The children ran into the kitchen where their mom was fixing their lunch. Lisa spoke for the group and told their mother what they had in mind. Mother thought that it would be all right as long as Ramor stayed with them all night. Of course, they would have to find Ramor first and see if this campout would fit into his plans. The children ate their lunch of vegetable soup and peanut butter and jelly sandwiches, with pickles and potato chips on the side. Everyone hurriedly ate everything and then put on their sweaters to go outside to find their friend Ramor.

As usual, they walked down the path to the large oak tree. They were excited by the prospect of camping out. They had wanted to go camping for a long time, but the opportunity never seemed to arise. Soon they were by the old oak tree, and in a jiffy their friend was right in front of them. He already had on his hiking clothes and had a little knapsack on his back.

"Where would you children like to go camping today? How about a little trip up into the mountains, just for the night?"

"Ramor," David said, "you just know everything. We'd love to go camping in the mountains."

"Get onto the magic carpet and hang on tight. Off we go!"

And off they went on the magic carpet, high into the sky and up above the puffy white clouds. In no time at all, they could see the outline of gentle rolling hills and mountains coming up ahead of them. Ramor set the carpet down right in the middle of a beautiful pine tree forest that was growing high up in the mountains. (It reminded Lisa and David a lot of the mountains they had seen in the movie *The Sound of Music*.) On the ground below the pine trees, there were lots of pine needles that made the ground soft and sort of slippery. Everyone sat down on the comfortable mat of pine needles for a little rest. Ramor asked if anyone was thirsty and took the children over to get a drink of fresh cold water that was seeping out of the ground in a nearby spring. The water tasted cool and refreshing.

Ramor found a good spot where everyone could pitch their tents. Each tent was big enough for two people. Lisa and Karen shared one tent, and David and Stacy shared the other. Ramor had his own little tent for himself. After the tents were pitched, the children laid pine bows on the floor of their tents to prevent the dampness of the ground from penetrating their sleeping bags. Ramor had brought along a down-filled sleeping bag for each child. They were very warm and comfortable.

The tents were set around a little open space where Ramor was going to start a fire for cooking supper. The children went to gather wood for the fire. Each child made several trips, and soon a nice stack of wood, mostly hickory, was gathered—enough to last the night. There was still time prior to supper before the sun would set.

The children joined hands and went to pick berries to eat with their breakfast. They also wanted to take some back to their mom.

The woods were filled with berries, and Ramor showed them which ones to pick, because some could be poisonous. They found mostly blueberries and huckleberries. They ate them as they picked, and it wasn't long before the buckets that Ramor had given them were filled to the brim. Everyone's mouth and hands were slightly blue from picking and eating so many berries.

The sun had started to set, and everyone was sitting around the campfire watching Ramor prepare supper. He was fixing a special "campers' stew." It's true that lots of children don't like stew, but being outdoors, the four children's appetites blossomed, and, besides that, the aroma from the bubbling stew pot smelled delicious. As they sat there, they looked up into the tall pine trees that almost seemed to reach to the sky. Every now and then they could see a blue jay dart from one tree to the next, and several squirrels came out onto the branches to watch the campers down below. The children were having a grand time. It was so good to be out of doors. The sun was about to set, and everyone put on their sweaters, because it was starting to get chilly.

Ramor brought plastic plates and spoons with them and passed them out when he was ready to dish up the stew. He also had hot dogs in reserve, just in case someone wanted to roast one. Everyone was so hungry, and they very much enjoyed eating the delicious food cooked outdoors. Somehow it just seemed to taste better than at home.

Suddenly they heard a noise and a tremendous crashing in the bushes behind them. It startled Lisa so much that she dropped the hot dog she was roasting right into the fire. They all turned around, and what do you suppose they saw?

Woodland Creatures

Everyone looked up from their dinner in the woods when they heard the noise—almost a crackling sound—in the forest around them. They were rather startled. It had been so quiet in the woods, and just the singing of the birds had previously been heard. The two little girls jumped up and ran over to be beside Lisa and David. Ramor told everyone to be calm, and they would go investigate the noise together.

On the edge of the clearing where they had been cooking was a large clump of bushes. They peeked through the bushes and saw a family of deer standing there. The deer had made all the noise crashing through the dense underbrush. There was a buck (the daddy) with large antlers; a doe (the mommy) somewhat smaller but very pretty—she was a soft brown with a shiny black nose and two very big, dark brown eyes; and two fawns (the babies), who had white spots all over their backs. One fawn was a boy and the other a girl. When the children saw them, they became very excited. The deer sensed that they were being watched, and the daddy started pawing the ground with his right hoof. This was a sign for them not to come any closer.

Ramor poked his head around the bush and walked out into the open so the daddy deer could see him. When the deer saw Ramor, they were no longer upset, and the whole family walked over to Ramor. Ramor was a friend of all the forest animals.

The deer told him that they had smelled the wonderful aroma of the food cooking in the little camp and came over to investigate. Ramor invited the family of deer to come over and share the food. Since the deer ate only vegetables, berries, and things like that, Ramor fixed a tremendous tossed salad for the deer family to enjoy. The children held out fresh carrots and lettuce and fed the deer right out of their hands. Everyone was having a good time feeding the deer family.

Lisa, David, Stacy, and Karen soon finished their dinner and supposed that they were the only children ever to have had a family of deer over for dinner. After everyone finished their main meal, they had fresh berries that the children had picked earlier for dessert. The deer just loved the huckleberries. After everyone was through, there was still enough sunlight for the deer family to show the children around the mountains.

Lisa, David, and Ramor walked, while Stacy and Karen rode on the back of the big buck. They went down an animal trail along which people had never before traveled. Soon other animals began to form a line, following closely behind the four children, Ramor, and the deer family. There were several rabbits, three chipmunks, about ten squirrels, a small red fox, and of all things, a friendly old black bear, lumbering down the trail bringing up the rear. That was quite a site to behold, this parade of people and animals marching together through the mountains.

Birds were flying overhead and chirping in the warm breeze. Soon they were at the tiptop of the mountain. There was an open meadow on the top, and they could all get a good look at the surrounding countryside. It was very beautiful. Down below in the valley they could see a stream winding its way toward a large lake.

From up so high, all the trees below looked small. There they were, four little children surrounded by the animal "critters," just enjoying the scenery. Ramor suggested that they get on back to the camp as the sun was rapidly setting, and it would soon be dark and cold in the mountains. Happily, they marched back to the campground together.

The black bear wandered over to the stew pot, and David poured the remainder out onto a large plate so the bear could eat it. Stacy threw scraps of bread out for the birds to eat, and Karen fed some peanuts, which they had brought with them, to the squirrels and chipmunks. Lisa was busy getting the sleeping bags in the tents ready for everyone to crawl into for a warm, comfortable night's sleep in the great outdoors. Soon the animals were all gone. Ramor said he would keep the fire going all night so that they would have warmth and light.

Everyone crawled into the tents and jumped into their warm sleeping bags. The next thing you heard was "Good night, Lisa"— "Good night, David"—"Good night, Stacy"—"Good night, Karen"— "Good night, Ramor." Not too much later, all the children were asleep in their tents, while the twinkling stars watched down on them from above.

The dawn came, and the children were awake with the rising of the sun. The fire was still going, the embers were glowing, and everyone gathered around to cook breakfast. There is nothing any better than bacon and eggs cooked outside over an open fire for breakfast. Ramor had even put on a pot of hot chocolate, as the air this early in the morning was still rather chilly. All four children washed and brushed their teeth in a nearby stream. When they came back, the bacon was sizzling. Lisa made a big pan of scrambled eggs for the group. They sat around on logs that they used for tables and chairs and ate until everything was gone.

"OK, children," said Ramor. "Gather up your things. It's time for us to return home. When you are ready, we'll hike down the mountain to our magic carpet and take off on it and head for home."

On the way down the mountain, David spotted a cave and wondered if they could investigate. Ramor told them to go ahead but to be careful. He would wait for them outside beside the magic carpet. David was in the lead this time, as he, Lisa, Stacy, and Karen went off to investigate the cave. They entered the cave. It looked like it went right down into the center of the earth. It was very, very dark, but on into the cave they marched.

The Cave

David led the way into the cave, with Stacy and Karen holding hands in the middle, and Lisa bringing up the rear so that no one would stray. It was rather dark, and it took a while for everyone's eyes to adjust, just having come from the bright sunlight. Not only was the cave dark, but it was also a little on the damp side, and you could see the roots of trees growing through the ground into the ceiling of the cave. The ground was hard and somewhat rocky. David had a good flashlight with him, and he shined the light in front of everyone so that they wouldn't stumble.

The cave seemed to wind deeper and deeper into the earth. The children kept on walking. Soon they heard a chirping noise and a strange rustling sound in the background. Up ahead they could see what appeared to be a dark cloud coming toward them. Lisa and David pulled Stacy and Karen behind a rock to take cover. Hundreds of tiny bats had seen the light from the flashlight and became disturbed. They began to fly out of the cave, passing overhead with a tremendous flapping sound.

"That sure was scary," said Lisa.

"I think they're gone now, and we shouldn't have to worry about them anymore," replied David. "Come on. Let's move on down the path farther into the cave."

The cave began to widen out just a bit and made walking easier. They could see somewhat better now, since their eyes had become more adjusted to the darkness in the cave. The walls of the cave were a myriad of colors and reminded the children of the colors of the Painted Desert. Lisa told the other children how she had driven through the Painted Desert with their mom and dad, and how she remembered the pretty colors of the Painted Desert from home movies she had seen. Lisa also told them that the pretty colors came from the minerals that are found in the soil, each coloring the earth a different shade.

Farther down the cave they started to see what looked like icicles hanging down from the ceiling and also growing up from the floor. It was very cool in the cave, but the children knew that it wasn't cold enough for ice to form. In deep caves the temperature stays the same year-round and is usually comfortable. David went up to one of the "icicles" that was coming up from the floor, and it was hard like the earth but felt slippery. What they had found were stalactites and stalagmites. As the water from the earth seeps through the ceiling of the cave, it drops onto the floor. Over hundreds of years, the water evaporates, and lime deposits build up on the ceiling in the shape of icicles; these are stalactites. The water drips onto the floor below and evaporates and more lime deposits form, building an icicle-like thing growing out of the floor; these are stalagmites. Just remember: tites grow down, and mites grow up. Looking at all the tites and mites reminded them of a city with many buildings topped by steeples and spires. The tites and mites were multicolored because of various minerals and were very beautiful. The children remembered seeing pictures from inside the Carlsbad Caverns in New Mexico that looked like this.

Lisa said, "I wish that I had brought my new camera with me so I could have taken pictures to show my school teacher. She would have enjoyed seeing this."

Soon they came to a large underground lake. There happened to be a boat beside the lake, and the children got in and began to row. They could see light in the distance and thought that perhaps it was another way out. Lisa took one oar while David took the other. Karen and Stacy sat quietly in the middle and watched. The lake was very still, but toward the middle they began to feel the current sweeping them on. Soon the current took control, and they could no longer guide the boat with the oars. All they could do was sit back and watch. The lake began to narrow, and they began to move faster and faster, up and down. It was like riding the Matterhorn at Disneyland all over again. What a thrill they were having!

Fortunately, the current carried the small boat around the rocks. They were moving so fast that everything around them seemed a blur. The water was white with foam. Soon the boat glided to a stop. Suddenly, they saw good old Ramor waiting for them on the shore. He was laughing and holding his sides. The children laughed, too. They had had such an exciting ride down the little underground river. They were a little wet and tired but had enjoyed every minute of it.

"OK, children," Ramor said, "let's get moving. It's time we headed for home. I have the magic carpet right here, and we can all jump on."

Off they went into the sky, high over the beautiful mountains, and flew back to their wonderful mother. She was anxiously awaiting them and was worrying just where the children had been. When they walked into the apartment, they started talking all at once, telling their mom about the wonderful camping trip, about all the animals they had seen, and about their trip into the cave.

Mother said, "That was just wonderful, children! Now, you go wash up, clean your teeth, and get ready for bed. It's late now, and you must be just exhausted. You can sleep late tomorrow. It's the first day of your spring vacation. Perhaps your friend Ramor will have something special for you to do over your holiday. Good night, everyone. I love you."

Circus

"Here it is, spring vacation, and we don't have anything to do," said David.

"I wish the rain would stop so at least we could go out and play with our friends," replied Lisa, "but it looks like it's going to last all day. I guess the April showers came early this year."

The toddlers were in the bedroom playing nicely with an old circus set that David had gotten when he was a little boy. There was a seal with a ball on his nose, and Stacy had built a little stand to hang monkeys on. They were having such a good time.

Lisa and David watched them for a while, and then Lisa said, "David, do you remember that circus we went to in Hawaii? When that man in the gorilla suit came up into the audience, you just jumped right into Daddy's lap. He sure was a horrible-looking creature. Remember they also had the Three Stooges, but I didn't think that they were as funny as they are on television. This sure would be a good day to go to a circus, wouldn't it?"

"How are we going to be able to ask Ramor to take us to a circus?" asked David. "It's still raining too hard to go down to our secret spot in the woods where we always meet him. Maybe if we all sort of sat together and thought real hard for him to come here, he would somehow be able to get our message. Stacy, Karen, come here into Lisa's room. We're going to try something."

All four children sat in a circle on the floor and held hands with one another and said softly, "Come on, Ramor." On about the sixth, "Come on, Ramor," they looked up, and there was good old Ramor sitting on the studio bed in Lisa's room.

"Mighty nice room you've got here, Lisa," he said. "I heard you thinking about me and came over as soon as I could."

"You mean you can hear our thoughts?" said Lisa.

"Of course," replied Ramor. "I have something called ESP—that's extrasensory perception—and whenever someone thinks about me real hard, his or her thoughts somehow float through the air and into my mind. I was thinking about you children today, anyway, and I thought that I would take you to visit a circus."

"Ramor," said David, "you always know what we have on our minds. We can't fool you. Stacy and Karen have never been to a real circus, and I know they are going to have fun."

In a twinkling of an eye and quicker than you can say "Jack Robinson," the children suddenly found themselves standing in front of the biggest circus tent they had ever seen. Ramor was with them and had a whole roll of tickets so they could all go inside and see and do everything. Both sides of the gates were marked with large red banners, and there was a large sign overhead that said, "Best Circus in the World."

The children could hear the circus music in the background, and every now and then they could even hear the roar of a lion. There were all sorts of things to ride on and hot dogs, cotton candy, peanuts, popcorn, Crackerjacks, and all kinds of other good children's food to eat and drink.

"Come on, children," Ramor said, "let's go inside. The show's about to begin and you children are going to be in it. I've talked to the circus owner and told him about you and how good you are at entertaining people. Now, don't you worry; I've given you magical powers that you don't even know you have. You'll be surprised at just how much you really can do. Come on, the dressing rooms are over this way."

The children were excited and wondered just what new magical powers Ramor had given them. When they got to their dressing rooms, costumes were laid out for the four children. There were three ballerina costumes for the girls and a strong man's costume for David.

"Get dressed quickly. You are just about to go on," announced Ramor.

Just then they heard the ringmaster (it was a three-ring circus) announce that the four children would be performing next in the center ring. They were all ready to go, but they weren't quite sure what they were supposed to do.

All three girls looked cute in pink ballerina costumes. They walked down the aisle and waited at the entranceway for David. David had put on a strong man's costume—a leopard skin outfit with a big, wide belt around his waist. He suddenly felt very strong, as though he could lift anything in the world.

In the meantime, the girls found out what they were to do. They were going to be bareback riders on three beautiful white ponies. All three girls jumped onto the ponies' backs and had no trouble at all standing there. Their balance was so good that they knew they couldn't fall off. They were ready! The three girls were standing on the ponies, and David was ready in his strong man's outfit. There was a flourish of the drums, a spotlight shone on the center of the ring, and everything was quiet. The announcer then said, "Introducing Lisa, David, Stacy, and Karen."

Ramor said quietly, "Good luck, children—you're on!"

The Big Show

The three girls rode into the center ring standing on the backs of three pretty white ponies that were prancing and strutting around. Lisa's pony was in the lead, with Stacy and Karen following. With the magical powers that Ramor had given them, their balance was so good that standing on the moving ponies was as easy as pie.

Meanwhile, David had come out into the center ring and walked up onto a platform in the middle of the ring. A spotlight was on him. The ringmaster announced that David would pick up a 500-pound weight that was on the floor of the platform. David felt the power surge through his muscles as he bent to pick up the iron weight. It was difficult to lift at first, but then he picked it up with one hand and held it high over his head. After this feat of strength, he put the weight down, and the crowd loudly applauded.

The ringmaster asked for a volunteer from the audience. A large man came onto the stage. David picked him up with both hands and held the man horizontally over his head. The crowd was amazed at the tremendous strength of the little boy on the stage. Everyone once again applauded his feat of strength.

The girls were still gliding gracefully about the ring on the backs of the ponies. The spotlight was now on them and followed the girls around the ring. An attendant had set up three large hoops in the ring, and the horses were to jump through the hoops. The girls would each have to duck to get through.

Suddenly the attendant set the hoops ablaze. The ponies, with the girls, were to jump through the burning hoops. A hush came over the crowd as they watched, spellbound. Stacy and Karen wouldn't have to bend over too much, but Lisa was getting so tall that she had to bend way down to ensure that she wouldn't bump the hoop with her head. One-two-three-go! Up and through. They made it! The crowd cheered wildly!

Now the ponies were side by side, and Stacy and Karen hopped over onto Lisa's pony with her. The three of them went round and round the ring together on the one pony as the crowd applauded. The pony slowed down as they jumped off and stood in the center of the ring and bowed.

Next the ringmaster announced that the four children would walk the high wire that was strung across the top of the big top. David was in the lead as they climbed the tall ladder leading toward the top of the tent. They climbed higher and higher. The people below looked very tiny, and the children could see everyone's faces looking upward. They knew that all eyes were upon them. At the top of the ladder was a platform where all four children could stand. At one end of the platform was the beginning of the high wire that ran across the tent to another similar platform on the other side.

The children slipped on special shoes to help them better keep their balance on the wire. Each child carried a small umbrella that would also help maintain balance. Onto the wire they went, slowly inching their way forward. David was in the lead, followed by Stacy and Karen, with Lisa bringing up the rear. It was so quiet in the tent that you could hear a pin drop. The farther out on the wire they went, the bouncier it became. Once David slipped off but caught himself and hung onto the wire with his bare hands. With his extra strength, he swung himself back onto the wire and kept going. Everyone in the crowd was breathless as they watched.

For a little added attraction, Lisa and David carried Stacy and Karen piggyback the last several steps of the way on the high wire. The crowd went wild over that. As they reached the opposite platform, another tremendous cheer went up from the crowd. When they came down the ladder, the announcer told the audience that there was more to come, and the fabulous four children were just getting started to entertain them. What would they do next? The crowd couldn't wait to see.

Clowning Around

The children went back into their dressing rooms to change costumes. A nice lady came in and dressed Stacy and Karen in clown costumes. She put great big ears on them, a round red nose, and great big shoes. Besides that they both had on cute, little plaid dresses. Lisa and David were both dressed in riding outfits with boots on. They gave David a gun (with blanks) and Lisa a long whip. Lisa and David wondered what they were supposed to do with these things.

The little sisters had already gone back out into the center ring and were having the best old time clowning around. Karen was trying to do a somersault, and Stacy was standing on her head. The whole crowd was laughing at how funny they looked.

Meanwhile, David and Lisa heard the ringmaster announce that they would now tame a cage full of savage beasts from the jungles of darkest Africa. A hush came over the audience as David and Lisa once again came out into the center ring. A big cage had been moved into the center ring. An entry door lifted, and six large lions ran down a chute and into the cage! They were stalking back and forth and walking in circles around the cage. The children somehow knew just what to do. They came over and opened the door of the cage and walked inside. The two little sisters nervously watched from the sidelines.

David fired the pistol into the air. The loud bang sounded deafening in the quiet tent. With the noise, all the lions backed into a corner. David held a chair in one hand, which he kept between himself and the lions. Lisa cracked her whip, and the lions immediately took their places on individual stands that were set up in a semicircle inside the cage. The crowd applauded. The lions each sat on their little stands. Lisa cracked the whip once again, and all the lions stood up on their hind legs. Once again the crowd applauded!

The lions were fierce looking animals, but somehow they seemed to sense that Lisa and David were in charge. David fired his gun once more—everyone jumped—and the lions dismounted from their stands and walked around the cage. With the crack of Lisa's whip, they came to the center of the cage and formed a pyramid of lions, the first time that this feat had ever been accomplished. Quickly, David fired his pistol into the air, and the lions raced back up the chute. The act was over. The crowd gave a standing ovation to the two brave children, and Stacy and Karen danced around in a circle holding hands.

The children now had time for only one more act. Quickly they changed clothes and prepared for the flying trapeze. Each child wore a long, flowing cape, which said on the back in large black letters "The Flying Four Children." Lisa and Karen went up a ladder to one high platform, and David and Stacy climbed the other one. David mounted one swinging trapeze bar, and Lisa was on the other. They each did a little flip and were hanging by their legs. They were swinging back and forth very gently to the tune of "The Man on the Flying Trapeze."

As Lisa swung back toward her platform, Karen jumped off and grabbed her by the hands. She wasn't even scared! All the children knew it must be magic, especially when she swung gracefully over toward David and did a little flip, and he caught her by the hands and deposited her on the platform on his side. Next Stacy grabbed onto David's hands and swung over and was caught by Lisa, who then placed her on the platform nearest her. Lisa stood on her bar as it went to and fro. She jumped off with a half twist, and David caught her with his hands while his legs were wrapped around his swinging trapeze bar. Her bar was still swinging back and forth as she jumped onto the platform beside Karen. Later, David, while standing on his own bar, jumped off and caught the bar that Lisa had just vacated. He had to make a tremendous leap to catch it, but he did! He then jumped onto the platform beside Stacy. After that, the children turned toward the audience and bowed. The crowd went wild! The children climbed back down the ladders and scurried off to their dressing rooms as the audience was still loudly applauding.

Ramor was there to greet them. He said, "Your mom and dad would have been very proud of you tonight if they could have just been here to see your performances. You were magnificent—of course, my little magic helped out a bit! I wouldn't advise you to climb into a lion's cage or fly on the trapeze when I'm not around. Hurry now and change back into your street clothes. We have to hurry home. You have been gone for quite a while now, and we don't want your beautiful mother to worry."

They were ready in no time, and Ramor, being a very nice man and knowing what all children like, bought them each a cotton candy cone before they left. Everyone looked a little fuzzy pink around the mouth when they arrived home. No wonder none of them were very hungry for dinner.

They excitedly told their mom of their adventure at the circus. It had all been very tiring, and all four children headed directly for their beds and quickly drifted off to sleep. Strangely, again they had the same dream. Ramor came to them and said he was going to take a little vacation himself, because he wanted to visit with his mother and father who lived far away. He felt that they would most certainly be in safe hands with their wonderful mother while he was gone. "I'm going to miss you good children," Ramor said, "but I'll see you again in two or three weeks. Have fun with your mom while I'm away. I love you all."

Haunted House

It was a beautiful, sunny day, a Friday afternoon. Mother had just picked up David from school, and they were both at home waiting for Lisa to come walking down the hill to the apartment. Stacy and Karen were out swinging on the swings. David decided he should water his vegetable and flower garden, because they were growing nicely since he had started taking such good care of them. The petunias were beginning to spread, and it seemed as though there were twice as many as when he had planted them. With plenty of sun and water, everything was growing abundantly. David had already dug several of his radishes and beets, and the fresh vegetables really were delicious.

It was still a little too chilly for swimming when Lisa got home, so Mother thought she would give everyone a treat and take all four children to Baskin-Robbins for an ice cream cone. Stacy and Karen both had single scoops of vanilla, and Mother, Lisa, and David each had a double cone of tutti-frutti and chocolate marshmallow. The ice cream was absolutely delicious. It wasn't long before it was all over the little ones' faces, and Mother had to clean them up. They finished their ice cream, and, since it was such a nice day and everyone was enjoying themselves so much, they decided to drive over to visit with Aunt Doris for a while.

They drove up the steep hill of the driveway, and everyone got out and went into the house through the basement. No one was at home except Aunt Doris and her dog, Snoopy—a little, brown dachshund. Aunt Doris gave everyone something to drink, because they were thirsty from the delicious ice cream that they had just finished eating. Mother and Aunt Doris sat down to talk, and the children played with Snoopy. Aunt Doris invited everyone to stay for hamburgers and said Uncle Freddie would cook them on the grill outside when he came home from work. It would be some time before supper would be started so Lisa, David, Stacy, Karen, and Snoopy went out into the backyard to play. As usual, Stacy and Karen headed for the swings, and Lisa and David played catch with a ball that David had brought with him. Snoopy ran back and forth as the ball went from side to side. In a little while, Stacy and Karen came over to Lisa and David. They wanted to do something else. Lisa suggested they surprise Mother and Aunt Doris and go into the woods behind the house and pick a bouquet of wildflowers for the dining room table. Everyone thought that it would be a good idea, and off everyone went, with Snoopy trailing along behind.

The farther they went into the woods, the darker it became as the leaves from the trees blocked out the sunlight. It was pleasant, though, and everything in the woods looked very, very green. There were many wildflowers along the way, and each child collected a bundle as they went along. They came to the crest of the hill and started down the other side. As they walked down the far side of the hill, they saw an old house in the distance. They had never noticed it before; you couldn't see it from Aunt Doris's backyard. It only came into view when you started down the backside of the hill. It was made of stone and was very large. It was shaped somewhat like a miniature castle. As they came closer, they could see that the windows were boarded up but decided they would go closer and take a peek inside. It was a rather spooky-looking place.

As they approached the house, everything became very quiet, and even the birds stopped singing. They stepped onto the front porch of the house and peeked inside the front door. There was furniture inside, but it was covered by sheets, and everything was dusty. They could even see cobwebs as the rays of golden sunlight bounced off each silver thread. Snoopy had been sniffing around the front door, and, the next thing the children knew, he had pushed it open and run inside.

The children all hollered, "Snoopy, Snoopy!" but he didn't come back.

"I guess we'll have to go in and find him," said David.

"It's a little scary," replied Lisa, "but we have to find Snoopy."

All four children held hands and went inside. Karen wandered over to an old piano and started banging on it and nearly scared everyone to death. Lisa pulled her away, and everything was quiet once again. Snoopy was nowhere to be seen. He had simply vanished. David spotted his footprints on the dusty floor, and the children started to follow them up the creaky staircase. At the top of the stairs were five doors, all closed. One was slightly open, and they could see the rays of sunlight coming through the partially opened door. Lisa peeked into the room. "You won't believe this," she said, "but there's a ghost in there!"

The other children wanted to see, too, so they peeked into the room and saw something white floating around. It was coming toward them. What were they to do?

A Ghostly "Tail"

The children galloped down the stairs and at the bottom stopped to peek over their shoulders to see if the ghost had followed them. There was nothing coming after them! Slowly they climbed back up the stairs to see where the ghost had gone. The poor light in the house, the covered furniture, and the dust and cobwebs everywhere made everything spooky.

Slowly, step by step, they went back to the room where they had seen the ghost. David went first and looked into the room and sure enough a white sheet was moving around the room. He got a little braver and went inside. Then he noticed a funny thing. There was a little tail sticking out from under the sheet. David went a little closer and pulled the sheet away. It wasn't a ghost after all. Snoopy was caught under a card table chair that had a sheet thrown over it. In trying to get out from under the chair, his foot caught in the sheet, and he was dragging the chair all over the room. He was so happy to see David that his little tail didn't stop wagging.

The three girls came up, and everyone laughed when they saw what was happening. But they weren't laughing for long, because they started to hear strange music. They didn't know where it was coming from, but it sure sounded weird. They ran out of the room, following the sound of the music. It seemed to be coming from the attic. Up the creaky attic stairs they crept, one child trailing behind the other. They opened the door to the attic, and in one corner was an old organ. The music was coming from it. It was rather peculiar. The keys were moving, and the music kept coming, but they couldn't see anyone sitting there playing. They knew for sure that this time there had to be a ghost. They moved in closer but still could see no one at the keyboard. Suddenly, there was a brilliant flash of light and a puff of smoke. When the smoke cleared, there was a little man standing there laughing, and who do you think that it was? Right, it was Ramor, and he had been playing a little trick on the children.

Stacy and Karen were so happy to see Ramor that they danced up and down.

"Hello, children," said Ramor. "I've missed you. I'm back now, and we can have more fun together. The next time you see me, I want you to have thought up an exciting adventure on which I can take you. We'll have a great time!" With that, there was another puff of smoke, and Ramor was gone. Not only was Ramor gone, but the whole house was gone. All four children were standing beside a large maple tree where there had once been a house. Ramor must have done the whole thing with his magical powers.

Just then, they realized they hadn't eaten and were getting very hungry. They could smell the hamburgers and hot dogs cooking on the outdoor grill, and it made their mouths water. Off they all went back up the hill, and soon Aunt Doris's house was in view. Everyone was sitting on the patio waiting for them to return. Snoopy led the way and every now and then looked back to make sure that the children were following. When they finally arrived, they were very excited and told their mom that they had just been with their old friend Ramor. All they could think about and talk about while they were eating dinner was their coming adventure. Where would Ramor take them next?

To the Stars

School was out, and Lisa, David, Stacy, and Karen were outside playing on the swings. Lisa and David were each pushing their little sisters on the swings, and they kept saying, "Higher! Higher!"

"If you go much higher, you will be up to the stars," Lisa told them.

David heard her and said, "Say, that would be a good idea, Lisa. We've never had an adventure to the stars. Ramor has taken us just about every other place. That's one place we have never thought about going. Why don't we take a quick swim in the pool now and after lunch find our friend Ramor and see if he will take us there. We had better not tell Mom what kind of adventure we have on our minds this time. She might worry. On second thought, she'd worry if we didn't tell her, so let's go see what she thinks about this idea."

They ran back into the house looking for their mom. She saw them coming and gave each child a hug as each one ran into the house. The children first mentioned going swimming, and Mom thought that it was warm enough, so they scampered into the bedroom to put on their swimsuits. David was ready in a flash and waited in the living room for his sisters. Sooner or later they were all ready, and Mom had also slipped into her suit and was coming out to watch them swim. They carried towels and even had inner tubes, so Stacy and Karen could float.

Just before they left, Lisa said, "Mom, after swimming and after our lunch, we thought that we would try to find our friend Ramor. He hasn't taken us on an adventure in quite some time."

"Where were you thinking of going this time?" asked Mom.

"To the stars," replied Stacy, with a big grin on her face.

"My," said Mom, "that sure is a long way to go for an adventure. How in the world would you expect to be back by supper time?"

"Ramor has magical powers, and I know he wouldn't keep us too long. He wouldn't want you to worry. He will just seem to make time stand still when we are away on our trip," replied Lisa.

"Please, Mom!" they all cried.

"Let's go swimming now," said Mom, "and I'll think about it and let you know my decision after our swim."

So down to the pool they went for a nice, refreshing swim. Lisa and David jumped right into the pool and swam all the way to the other side. Mom helped Stacy and Karen into the pool, and they climbed into their inner tubes and began to swim and kick all around the shallow water. David and Lisa were practicing their diving for a while, and Stacy was holding onto her mom's hands while she pulled Stacy through the water. They were playing "motorboat." Karen accidentally splashed water into her own face, and Lisa ran to get a towel to wipe the water out of her little sister's eyes. They were all having such a good time. The sky was blue, it was a sunny and warm day, and everyone was happy. It wasn't too long before they started to get hungry, so they hopped out of the pool and raced back to the apartment for lunch.

Lisa said, "Mom, how about grilled cheese sandwiches? We haven't had that for a while."

Mom said, "Who wants tomatoes on their sandwich?"

Lisa and David wanted some on theirs, but Stacy and Karen wanted theirs plain. They ate everything on their plates, and then the little girls took a short nap. Even Lisa and David lay down and rested a while, since they knew that big things were in store for them after they found Ramor. Their mother had just given them permission to take a journey to the stars if Ramor was willing to take them!

It wasn't long before everyone was up and on their way outside. As usual, they were all holding hands and heading down their familiar path in search of the old oak tree where they knew that they could always contact Ramor. There were pretty flowers growing all along the path now, and the water in the creek was so clear that one could easily spot the minnows and tadpoles swimming around. David stopped for a minute to look at the water and saw a crayfish scurry along the bottom and hide behind a rock. On they went until, at last in the distance, they could see the old oak tree. Ramor was sitting beneath the old oak tree just waiting for them. He was eating an apple and relaxing, knowing that his friends were on their way to see him once again.

"Hi, Ramor," they called out.

"Hi, children," he answered. "I sure have missed you these past few days. I thought you were never going to get here. I've arranged a little trip for us to take among the stars, and it really will take some doing to get you back in time for supper. I've added rockets to my magic carpet, and that will speed things up a bit. OK, now, everyone onto the magic carpet. I've added seat belts for this ride."

Everyone strapped in.

"Let's all start the countdown together," said Ramor. "Five-Four-Three-Two-One," and off they blasted for the distant stars!

They wouldn't just stop at the moon but would also visit other far-off planets. They would be the first children in outer space! Off they zoomed!

Moon People

Everyone held on tightly as the four children and Ramor blasted off on the magic carpet for outer space. Just as on other trips on the magic carpet, everything below on the planet Earth began to get smaller and smaller. The trees, the houses, the cars, everything looked like miniatures. Suddenly, everything got cold, white, and bumpy. The carpet had gone through a cloud, but, in just a short instant, they were out of the cloud and still going higher and higher into the sky. The sky itself was becoming bluer and bluer. When they looked down again, all they could see was the puffy, white clouds that looked like a beautiful, soft carpet beneath them. It didn't seem like they were going as fast as they had been, so they relaxed their grip on the side of the carpet just a little. They kept on going up, up, higher and higher. Fortunately, through Ramor's magic they were able to breathe and didn't have to wear any special pressure suits, as did the astronauts; otherwise they would not have been able to withstand the freezing cold and reduced atmospheric pressure of outer space. With Ramor by their side, they had nothing at all to worry about. He was taking good care of them. Soon they looked down again, and the Earth looked like a small round ball far below. Up ahead they could see old Mr. Moon, and he was becoming larger and larger.

Lisa asked, "Ramor, is our first stop the moon?"

He answered, "Yes, I have some friends there I want you to meet. No one from Earth has ever met them. They are very shy creatures and hide whenever astronauts land on the moon. You will be the first people from Earth to meet them."

Everyone was getting excited to see what the moon was really like. They had heard about it so much lately, and at last they could see for themselves what the moon was really made of.

Ramor told them to hold on, because they were coming in for a landing. Bump! Thud! They were down. They gazed around. The moon looked barren and desolate, just like in the pictures they had seen. They got off the carpet, dusted themselves off, and proceeded to explore. As they walked, they could see the trail of footsteps they were leaving in the powdery dirt behind them. They soon realized that the force of gravity was much less on the moon than it was on Earth (since the moon is so much smaller than the Earth) and consequently they weighed much less and could jump very high into the air. They were all leaping around like a pack of kangaroos, having a grand old time.

Ramor calmed them down, because he wanted to take them on a walk to find his friends, the Moon people. The walking was getting a little rougher now. They had several large hills to climb, and there were many boulders in their way, spread around the tops of the hills. The air was chilly, but it didn't seem to bother the children. Soon they came upon a huge mound of boulders, almost like a mountain. Their way was blocked, and they couldn't go any farther.

Suddenly, David spied something looking at him from behind one of the large rocks. He pointed toward the boulder and said, "Ramor, what's that?"

Ramor answered, "Be very quiet. We don't want to scare him away—it's one of the Moon people."

They were able to get a better look now. It was a little green man no bigger than Ramor, about as tall as Stacy. He had two large antennae sticking out of his head. The Moon people use these to hear with, and they could even hear a pin drop. They had no ears. The little man had a rather large head and no hair. He was wearing a shimmering gold suit. His legs were shiny, and he had on short pants and bright red shoes. He quickly looked the other way, hoping no one would see him. Of course, everyone now was looking at him, and he was very embarrassed.

Ramor went over to him first, and introduced himself. Once the little man learned who Ramor was, all was well. Every one of the Moon people had heard of Ramor and respected him. Ramor took the little green Moon man over to the children and introduced each one to him. He was still rather shy and kept his eyes down on the ground. He spoke a rather funny language (full of *X*'s and *Z*'s), but through Ramor's magic, they were able to understand him just fine.

He said that the Moon people were having a celebration that day and hoped the children would come and visit with them. He said the Moon people had never seen Earth children, only astronauts, and the Moon scientist in particular would be eager to meet them. All they would have to do would be to follow him, and he would take them to Moon City, just across Moon River.

Off they went, hand in hand, following the Moon man to the Moon City on the other side of the Moon River. They wondered what it would be like. They were now following the little man onto a narrow ledge that ran up the side of the rocky mountain. Once they reached the top, they were able to see for miles and miles on the other side. What they saw was spectacular, absolutely the most beautiful sight they had ever seen.

Moon City

Moon City was very beautiful. Everything had somewhat of a greenish glow to it. The green was a very relaxing color and pleasing to the eyes. Everything in Moon City was round—all the houses, all the moon-mobiles, and even all of the swimming pools and tennis courts. They were walking down the rocky mountain into Moon City, and, the closer they got, the more they had the feeling that things weren't quite right. They were soon to have their suspicions confirmed.

They stopped for a short rest before proceeding farther and sat down beside some green rocks. David leaned up against one of the rocks and realized the rock was not hard like rocks on Earth but was of a rubbery consistency. It was very comfortable to lean against. The little green Moon man noted David's surprise.

The Moon man said, "David, break off a piece of that rock and take a taste."

David looked at the Moon man with surprise and took a little nibble of the rock. To his delight, it tasted very good. All the other children wanted to know what it tasted like. He told them that it tasted just like the most delicious cheese he had ever eaten. He had always heard that the moon was made of green cheese, and now he believed it. The other children broke off small pieces of rock (I mean cheese) and started to eat it, too. On the moon it turns out that green cheese is the main diet of everyone. That is what gives Moon people (and their Moon dogs) their green color. When Moon babies are born, they are a soft light shade of green and, as they grow older, they become a very beautiful shade of deep green. Of course, the moon is only made of cheese in this special moon valley. All other parts of the moon are just barren rocks, as we know rocks to be here on Earth.

Not only are the moon rocks (cheese) edible, but they can be cut like lumber since moon trees are too skinny for boards. Moon people build their houses out of it. They make some of their houses very quickly by hollowing out a large moon rock. That's one reason why all of the moon houses are circular. The Moon people can also melt down the cheese and pour it into molds to make their moon-mobiles. They must make these in a circular shape, because liquid moon cheese only hardens in circular form. It's because of this that Moon people always do things and build things in circles. They find it difficult to stray from their city, because they always walk in circles and eventually wind up where they began. Occasionally a Moon person wanders outside of the valley, and that's how they acciden-tally saw the astronaut who landed on their planet (moon). Of course the Moon people do a lot of flying in their circular flying sau-cers and have visited far-off places such as the Earth and other planets in the solar system. Every now and then here on Earth we hear of flying saucers with little green men, and they are most prob-ably reports of these friendly, shy Moon people.

So the children, Ramor, and the Moon man walked on down into Moon City. That day was a special day in Moon City. They were hav-ing a bouncing contest. As I said earlier, on the moon a person can jump very high, because the pull of gravity is much less than it is on Earth. Champion jumpers from all over the city had assembled in the "circular square" for the contest.

Lisa said, "David, you're a good jumper. Why don't you enter? I'll bet you could win."

He replied, "Well, Lisa, if you think I've got a chance, I'll go ahead and enter."

In all there were ten little green men in the contest, plus David. Lisa, Stacy, and Karen stood on the sidelines cheering for their brother. David jumped twelve feet into the air, higher than the little Moon men had ever seen anyone jump. They awarded him the winner's trophy right then and there.

After the contest, they gathered around tables set with all kinds of delicious cheese. By this time, it was getting rather late, and the sun was beginning to set. When the sun sets on the moon, it gets extremely cold so everyone goes into their little round, warm, cheese houses. That night the children had a most wonderfully sound sleep and awoke the next morning exceedingly refreshed.

Ramor stood in the door of their moon house and said, "OK, children, let's get moving. We're all getting a ride in a flying saucer and taking a tour of the solar system. Each one of us will have our own Moon ship, and a Moon man (or woman) will be flying each one. We'll pick up our magic carpet when we get back to the moon."

After a quick breakfast of special cheese (naturally), they were on their way. Each child met their Moon man driver and was led to a flying saucer. They were all lined up in a circle—five flying saucers—ready to take off after each child was safely aboard.

The Solar System

Each flying saucer (green in color, naturally) took off straight up. There was a round, plastic dome (really made of thin cheese) on top of each saucer, and each child could see out all around. The Moon men drivers were very friendly and smiled at the children. Xenoph was the name of David's driver, and he let David sit at the controls and fly the spacecraft. David zipped it up and down, round and about, and practically inside out. The girls were watching David fly from their saucers and were amazed at how well he was able to maneuver about the sky. Flying in the saucers made them feel free as birds sailing in the wind.

Their first stop was to be the brightest planet in the solar system, Venus. As they approached Venus, they could see swirling clouds all around the planet. The five saucers sat down on what appeared to be a desert area. The winds were blowing so strongly that they decided not to get out of their spacecraft. There were no people on Venus, but there were many peculiar-looking plants growing in this desert-like part of this strange, strange world. Suddenly the wind became so intense that it started to rock the spaceships. They decided they had better take off before their crafts were damaged from flying debris. Venus had not been too hospitable.

They headed to another planet called Pluto, the outermost planet of the solar system, and one that people knew very little about. They were on their way when all the Moon men began chattering excitedly to one another and pointing behind them. The children (and Ramor) looked back, and, in the distance, they could see several red-colored space vehicles pursuing them. What was it all about?

From his space vehicle, Ramor told the children over the radio (there was a radio set in each saucer) that it seemed that the red spacecraft were from the war planet Mars (sometimes called the red planet because it has a reddish glow when seen from Earth). The Martians were the troublemakers of the galaxy and were considered sky pirates.

The Moon people were well known for their fine spaceships. The five Moon craft surged forward all at once and left the red Martian craft in their space dust. They could attain speeds that approached the velocity of light.

The Martians didn't give up easily but kept on coming. The computers in their spacecraft had already plotted the Moon men's machines on their course for the planet Pluto. Zip, over the thousands of miles toward Pluto they raced; they were traveling 180,000 miles per second (the speed of light is 186,000 miles per second). No one had ever gone that fast before. The Moon men were pushing their flying saucers to the limit. At that speed, time was practically standing still as they were "here" and "there" almost at the same time.

Now they were hovering over Pluto, a cold and dark planet (and naturally it was shaped just like a dog—just kidding). It really got its name from the King of the Underworld, Pluto or Satan, because so little was known about this inhospitable planet. Once on the ground, they shuttled their saucers behind the large rocks that dotted the surface of the dark planet. Everyone scampered out and congregated with Ramor to determine a course of action. They knew that the mad, mean, maniacal Martians were still on their way to hunt them down.

Ramor had the situation well under control! He said, "Children and Moon people—have nothing to fear, as I am going to create an 'optical illusion' that will fool the Martians. Now, here's what I'm going to do."

Optical Illusion

The Martians were coming, and something had to be done quickly. As the Martian spacecraft came closer, everyone could see that each spacecraft was fiery red in color, and the Martians inside looked mean. Their skin was copper-colored. They were bigger than the Moon men, with big heads and large, round eyes. They could see exceedingly well and were searching for the Moon men and the children. They had hoped to take them prisoner and take them back to their "war planet," Mars.

Ramor came to the rescue with more of his magic. With a snap of his fingers, he caused the entire planet of Pluto to be covered with dense clouds and fog. He then created an optical illusion of another planet that looked just like Pluto but was made only of thin air. He did it with a little machine he carried that took a laser picture of the planet. The picture is called a holograph. It is like taking a picture of a person, and you can see all around the person's projected image, but when you touch it, it is just thin air.

The Martians were confused when they saw the clouds around Pluto, but when they saw the holograph, they thought that it was the real planet and tried to land on it. As they came in for a landing, they just went right on through the planet since it was like landing on thin air. They kept trying and trying and never could quite figure out what the problem was. Finally the Martians thought that they would give it one more try and made a wide orbit. This time their orbit carried them into the clouds that surrounded the real planet Pluto. The last thing that they had suspected was to find mountains beneath those clouds, but they did! It was too late, and one of the Martians crashed his ship into the ground. The others flew back to Mars. Their wrecked spaceship skidded to a halt not too far from where the children and the Moon men were hiding. Lisa and David ran over to the wreckage of the rocket ship to try to pull the Martians to safety. Even though the Martians were mean, Lisa and David did their best to rescue them. The younger children watched from a distance. There were two Martians in the spacecraft, and they had been knocked out by the impact of their sudden stop. The Martian men weren't too big and were rather light, so Lisa pulled one to safety while David pulled out the other. They had to hurry, because the spaceship was starting to burn. They carried the Martians to the safety of the rocks just before the spaceship exploded.

In a little while the Martians awoke and realized what had happened. They were very grateful to the children for having saved their lives. It wasn't long before they were all talking to one another, and the Martians and the Moon men found they had much in common. They talked mostly about rocket ships. The Martians were worried that they wouldn't be able to get back to their planet Mars.

The Moon men graciously offered to take them back to Mars. They were curious to see the "Red Planet," because they had never been there. The Martians felt that once Moon people and Martians got to know one another, the Martians would forget their thoughts of war and would become good friends with all the people of the solar system. They went so far as to discuss setting up monthly meetings to work out problems.

It was starting to get cold on Pluto, and the children had spent more than their allotted time away from home. Ramor thought it was time to get started back to Earth. In no time, they zipped back to the moon (the Moon men would take the Martians back to their planet later on). Stacy sat in one Martian's lap, and Karen sat in the other Martian's lap. After they arrived back in Moon City, they had more good green cheese for a snack and then gathered around Ramor's magic carpet, getting ready for their trip back home. Everyone fastened their safety belts and waved to the Moon people as they took off on their journey back to Earth.

When the children arrived home, it was already dark, and their mom was beginning to worry. She was very much relieved when she saw the four of them come marching home hand in hand. The children ate supper, had their baths, put on their pajamas, and were ready for bed.

There was a full moon that night, so they went into Lisa's room to look at it. They shut off the lights and opened the curtains. It was a beautiful sight to behold. The Moon was so bright that they could clearly see the face of the "Man in the Moon." Once, they even thought they saw little green people walking about.

When Mom came to tuck them in, Karen and Stacy said, "We went to the moon!"

David said, "The Moon men are now my good friends! Mom, please buy some green moon cheese for us tomorrow."

Lisa was just about asleep. When her mom came in, she said, "I love you," and then fell fast asleep.

The Farm

It was a bright sunny summer day. Lisa was home from Girl Scout camp, and David had just finished up at day camp. No one could go in the swimming pool today, so the four children were sitting in the house wondering what their day would have in store for them. David was telling Lisa how much he enjoyed riding the horses at day camp, and she agreed that riding horses was fun. She had a chance to ride while at Girl Scout camp. They agreed that it would be fun to go horseback riding again.

Their mom overheard the conversation and said, "How would you four children like to visit a farm today? Perhaps they will have ponies there that you could ride."

All four children enthusiastically said yes, they would like to go.

Mom said, "Don't forget to take a bathing suit. I'm sure there's a lake where you can swim. We might even spend the night. I'll pack a picnic lunch for us. Let's get busy!"

Well, you should have seen them get busy. Everyone, including Mom, was excited, and it wasn't too long before they were ready to go, and it wasn't even yet nine o'clock in the morning.

They went to the car, and Stacy and David got into the rear of the station wagon while Lisa and Karen sat in the back seat. Poor Mom was up front all by herself. She drove down the highway, and they were enjoying the beautiful day with all of the windows down in the car. Everyone's hair was blowing in the breeze, but it was fun, the beginning of what was sure to be a fun day. Soon Mom turned off the main highway onto a dirt road that led into the countryside.

In a little while, they came to a small country town with a small theater and a grocery store in the old Town Square. Just the other side of town, a sign told them it was three miles to Mitchell Farm. Soon they began to see white fences surrounding the meadows with cows and horses grazing in the fields. Mom turned off the road and drove up to Mitchell Farm. She parked the station wagon beside the house in front of a large white barn.

Mrs. Mitchell was home so Mom went up on the porch to talk with her. The children were already exploring the barn. In the barn were cows, chickens, and some rabbits. The children were looking at a cow with big brown eyes. They patted her on the nose.

She looked at them and said, "Will you pass that bale of hay over here, please?"

The children couldn't get over that this was a talking cow.

Of course, they brought the hay over, and the cow said, "Thank you." She was polite, too.

She looked at the children and said, "You look surprised. All of the animals on this farm can talk. Most anyone can hear animals talk if you have the right kind of ears, and you children have the perfect ears for it." She then swished a fly off her back with her long tail.

All David could say was "wow," and Lisa, Stacy, and Karen were too flabbergasted to say much of anything.

"You children are all alike," the cow said. "The ponies are out back, and I know you are just dying to ride them."

The cow didn't have to say it again. The four children ran out through the back door of the barn and found two ponies saddled up and ready for riding. David and Lisa tried them first, while Stacy and Karen watched.

David heard a voice say, "Hold on tight." He looked around and said, "Who said that?" There was no one there.

"I did," the voice said, "and my name is Cecil."

David slowly looked down at his pony, and he knew at once who was talking.

"What's your name?" Cecil asked. David introduced himself and the other three children to the pony.

The other pony was shy and didn't talk much, but Lisa was kind to her and gave her some oats to eat. In a quiet voice the pony said, "My name is Louise."

All four children said, "Hi, Louise."

They rode the ponies around for a while, and then Karen got on the pony with David, and Stacy got on with Lisa. They were really enjoying themselves when they heard Mom calling them from the house. They told the ponies they would see them later and walked over to the pretty, yellow farmhouse with white shutters on the windows and flower boxes all around filled with begonias and daisies.

Mrs. Mitchell was a grandmotherly lady and was very, very kind.

Mom said, "Mrs. Mitchell has a surprise for you all—homemade ice cream. We have to help her make it, though, and each of you will take your turn at the handle of the ice cream maker. You have to turn it quite a bit so the ice cream will harden."

After about thirty minutes everyone had a sore arm, but it was worth it. The ice cream was delicious. It was vanilla ice cream with fresh, cut-up peaches in it. Mrs. Mitchell's farm had many peach trees, and she said the children could pick a basketful of peaches to take home with them.

Everyone was sitting on the porch of the farmhouse when Lisa suggested going swimming. They got their suits on (including Mom) and went down to the lake on the other side of the farm. It wasn't too far from the main house. There was a sandy beach with small stones scattered around. They had fun looking for smooth, flat stones that they could skip across the water. David threw one that skipped five times before it went "plop" into the water. They swam a while and were having the best time.

"You know," Mom said, "we never did eat our picnic lunch, so I've got a good idea. We'll just have a picnic supper here beside the lake, and for a good surprise we'll spend the night here on the farm. Mrs. Mitchell said she had plenty of room for us." Everyone was so excited! It was just a perfect day.

The Well

It was late in the afternoon now. The sun was still up, but the weather had cooled a bit. Everyone was hungry and eager for a picnic down by the lake. They still had their bathing suits on, including Mom, and were carrying the food, which was in bags and the lunch basket, from the car. There was a large, redwood picnic table beside the lake. Mom spread a nice red-and-white-checkered cloth over the table, and Stacy and Karen helped her set places for everyone. Lisa was pouring lemonade, and David was helping Mom put the food on the table which included potato salad and fried chicken, and, boy, did it look delicious! There were also potato chips, olives, pickles, and Mom's wonderful homemade chocolate cake for dessert. Lisa cut the cake and gave everyone a generous serving.

After the picnic, the children wanted to take a swim, but they had to wait a while before they could go in so their dinner would settle in their tummies. While they waited, they played catch with a rubber ball that they had brought. After a few kicks, the ball landed—kerplunk—in the water. David said he would get the ball when it was time to go swimming. They sat around and sang songs, and each child chose his or her favorite song for everyone to sing. After a while, the waiting time was up, and it was time to go into the water. Mom watched Stacy and Karen in the shallow water. They built sandcastles, while Lisa and David practiced their swimming. The ball had drifted out quite far now, and Lisa and David decided to race out to see who could get to it first.

Just as they reached the ball, they noticed that the water was going round and round and started getting faster and faster. They were both holding onto the ball to stay afloat. Both were tired from their swim out to the ball. It was all that they could do to hold on. They were going round and round, faster and faster, and they suddenly realized that they were also going down, down, down. They were trapped in a whirlpool!

No amount of kicking or paddling would free them, and they sank further and further into the water. They hit the bottom of the whirlpool with a thud, and both lost their grip on the ball. It rocketed out of their hands and back to the surface of the water, but they stayed down below! They held their breath, and both started to swim underwater. Everything was getting dark as they felt the undercurrent drawing them along the bottom of the lake. Soon, they were in a kind of narrow channel, and finally they popped to the surface, gasping for air. It was dark where they came up, but they could see a little light ahead. They swam faster as the current carried them downstream.

Soon they came to a ledge alongside the water, but they could tell they were still underground. They climbed onto the ledge and walked onward toward the source of the light. When they reached the end, they looked up and could see a bright moon and stars shining down on them. As they looked up, it was as though they were looking into a chimney, but it wasn't a chimney. They were down in the bottom of a well and looking up! The water from the lake had rushed underground, forming an underground tunnel. It finally came out where the old well had been dug into the ground long ago.

The next problem was to get to the top. The sides of the well were slippery, and they weren't having much success in climbing. Finally,

Lisa found what looked to be small steps on the side of the wall that led to the top.

"Stay here, David," she said, "and when I get to the top, I'll get help so we can get you out."

"Lisa," he replied, "when you reach the top, just lower the bucket, and then you can crank me to the top. It'll be easy."

"OK," she said, and off she scampered like a monkey to the top of the well.

When she reached the top, she lowered the bucket. David jumped onto the bucket, straddling the rope between his legs, and holding on tightly. Lisa started cranking him to the top. It was a long, hard job, and, by the time David arrived at the top, Lisa was pooped. Out he jumped, and they both ran back to the lake to tell Mom they were OK.

Their mom was worried to death. She had not seen Lisa and David swim out after the ball and thought that they had just been exploring in the nearby woods. She had not realized what had happened to them but was certainly relieved to see them all safe and sound. She hugged and kissed them as they told her their wild tale. She bundled them up and took them to the farmhouse where everyone was spending the night. They would drive back to the city in the morning. All four children were sleeping in the same room in one tremendously big bed. The lights were out, and everyone was ready to go to sleep.

They pulled the covers up around their noses, but Stacy said, "Lisa, I see two big eyes looking at us!"

Lisa poked her head out and said, "Stacy, you're right! What could that be?"

Who!

The eyes seemed to get bigger and bigger in the dark. All four children were huddled under the covers. Lisa said, "Do you see what I see?"

David had just fallen asleep. He rubbed his eyes, and then he, too, saw the two big eyes staring at them. "Who do you think it is?" he whispered.

It was very quiet in the room. Stacy and Karen were also wide awake and looking into the big eyes. They were a little scared and pulled the sheet up over their heads.

"Who's there?" Lisa asked. All they heard in reply was "Who-oo-oo."

Now what has big eyes and says who-oo-oo?

"I know what it's got to be," said David, "but how did an owl get into our bedroom? We left the window open, and he must have flown in. Let's get up and see just what is there."

The four of them got up and switched on the lights. Sure enough, there was a big owl perched on the end of their bed, winking his big old owl eyes.

"Turn off that light!" the owl said.

The children were so surprised to hear the owl talk that they immediately complied and snapped the light off.

"The light hurts my eyes, and I can see much better in the dark," The owl said. "Thank you."

"Gosh," said David, "we've found a talking owl."

"No," said the owl, "I've found you. I saw you down around the lake today. I was sleeping in a tree, and you woke me up. I usually sleep in the daytime and stay up all night. You looked like such nice children that I thought I would drop by and say hello. I'm a hoot owl, and my name is Who. You all said, 'Who's there?' and I replied, 'Who,' which is my name. It's really very confusing. I'm just one more of the animals around this farm that can talk. We only talk with friendly children, and every now and then grown-ups, but not very often. Most of us owls are wise old birds. We can talk and are also very smart. We know when to keep quiet, and sometimes that takes quite a bit of wisdom. We also know all about forest creatures, and, whenever they have troubles, they come to us to help them solve their problems. Each farm in these parts has at least one owl to help out the farm animals with things that might come up. How much longer will you children be staying on Mrs. Mitchell's farm?"

"We'll be leaving in the morning," answered Stacy.

Stacy and Karen had walked over to the bird and ran their hand down his back to feel the soft brown and white feathers. It was certainly surprising to find a bird that could talk, but the Mitchell farm was full of surprises.

The owl, Who, wanted to take the children around the farm at night, but the weather was a little chilly, so Lisa thought they had better not go outside. Who then offered to bring some of the night creatures up to the room to meet them. The window was wide open, and the owl flew out. In a jiffy, he was back, and a whole swarm of lightning bugs was right behind him. They made the room so bright it was almost like sunlight. The children sat on the bed, fascinated, while the lightning bugs performed for them. They made intricate patterns as they flew around the room. As a grand finale, they spelled each of the children's names in turn. These were rather clever lightning bugs; they could spell. It was just like a Fourth of July display.

In a flash they were gone, and the children waited to see what would be next. It was very quiet in the room as they waited, and the owl told them to be still, because the next visitor, another night creature, was very, very shy. They didn't see anything, but soon, from somewhere in the room, they heard the beautiful song of a bird. It was probably one of the softest and prettiest melodies they had ever heard. In a distant corner of the room they could make out a small bird silhouetted in the moonlight. It was standing on the chest of drawers and singing away. The bird was reddish-brown with a gray-white breast. It was a beautiful nightingale named Charlie, and a very rare bird at that. The children enjoyed the singing so much that they applauded when the little bird finished, but the sudden noise frightened him, and he flew away, right out of the window.

By this time, it was getting very late, and Karen and Stacy had just about fallen asleep. Who the owl said he still had to make his rounds of the farmyard and had to be on his way. He flew out the window and into the night. Everyone then crawled back under the covers and went fast asleep.

They were up bright and early the next morning and went down to the kitchen for breakfast. First they had cereal with freshly cut-up peaches and fresh milk, and then each had a helping of pancakes to eat. The outdoor farm life had given them wonderful appetites. After breakfast they helped their mom pack up the station wagon. As they pulled out of the driveway, they waved farewell to Mrs. Mitchell. She told them to be sure and come back to visit any time they wanted.

It was a long drive back home, and they were all glad to see their apartment once again. They just couldn't remember the last time they had had so much fun. Visiting this farm was something they would never forget and would have to do again very soon.

Honey Bee

The summer was drawing to a close, and the children were looking forward to going back to school to see their friends again. Stacy was going to start nursery school. Karen was going to stay home this year and keep her mom company. The children were hoping, though, that they would still have a few more adventures with their friend Ramor, so they would have more wonderful tales to tell their school-mates.

They had not been down by the old oak tree for a while, so they thought that they would get up early the next morning and head into the woods right after breakfast. They knew their friend would not let them down, and he might have something exciting in store for them. They were up bright and early the next morning. Their mom knew they had something special in mind because they dressed and ate their breakfast in no time at all.

"Children, be back by supper time if you are with your friend Ramor, otherwise come home in time for lunch. You all be careful. I'll see you sweet children later on this afternoon."

They went off hand in hand down the path that followed along-side the narrow stream. The morning was cool, and dewdrops were still on the grass. The air smelled fresh, and the birds were singing happily in the trees. It was a great morning to be alive. It was the beginning of another good day. Soon they were rounding the bend and saw the old oak tree in the distance. As they came closer, they spied their friend Ramor sitting on the lowest branch (it was still high off of the ground) and munching on an apple while reading a book.

"There you are," he said. "I've been waiting for you. I brought you apples to eat. These are rather magical red apples and don't be surprised what happens after you eat them."

The apples were the best the children had ever tasted. They sat on the grass beneath the tree and relaxed while they ate. At first they didn't notice anything happening, but in a few minutes everything around them started to get much larger. They realized that things weren't growing, but they were shrinking, just as had happened in their adventures with the ants. This time there was one added difference. They each had sprouted a pretty pair of blue, green, and yellow bee wings coming out from the middle of their backs.

David tested his wings first, and, the next thing he knew, he was flying all around the place. He tried a couple of flips, and those even worked. It was easier than swimming. The air was holding him up just as though he was floating in water. He could glide around like a bird or buzz around like a bee. It was a lot of fun; in fact, he couldn't remember doing anything more fun.

The three girls began to fly around, too, and started a game of tag, buzzing all around the big oak tree. Soon they were back on the ground waiting for Ramor to see what else he had in store for them. All the flying around didn't even seem to tire them out. They were ready to go at it again.

"Well, children," said Ramor, "I see that you are all checked out with your new wings. Why, even the birds don't fly any better than you do. I want you to look way up in the top of this old oak tree and tell me what you see."

Lisa strained her eyes and looked as hard as she could, but Stacy could see best of all because she was wearing her new glasses. "I see a big hole in the tree," she replied.

"You're right," answered Ramor, "and inside that hole is a bee-hive containing the finest honey bees in the world. They make the purest and sweetest honey you have ever tasted. It's particularly good on hot biscuits for breakfast. I thought that you would like to take a look at it and meet the queen bee. She's in charge of the whole hive. Are you ready now? Just follow me, and up, up, up we will go."

They flew to the uppermost branches of the tree and waited outside the beehive while Ramor went in. In just a few minutes, a whole swarm of honeybees flew out of the hive and swarmed around the children. There was such a loud buzzing noise that the children had to put their fingers in their ears to block it out. These were the worker bees that made the honey after they gathered nectar from the sweet-smelling flowers.

Once the honey was made, it was deposited onto the honey-comb walls of the beehive. The honeycomb walls inside the hive were hexagonal (six-sided) in shape. The outside of the hexagon was wax, and the inside was thick with honey. This made a secure home for the bees and was of a very strong and sound construction. In one part of the hive was the throne room for the queen (only one queen per hive) and adjoining it was the royal nursery. Just beyond the nursery and at the end of a long hallway were the hundreds of honeybees that produced the honey. It was all very interesting to see. Not many people have the opportunity to visit the inside of a beehive.

Soon the queen bee came out and buzzed her greeting to Ramor and the children. She had some of the bees pass out wax plates filled with honey cakes. A little pot of honey was set on a small side table. The children ate the cakes and dipped them into the honey they had poured onto their plates. It was delicious.

The queen took them into the nursery afterward so they could see the baby bees all clustered together. They were in eggs waiting to be hatched. The queen asked the children if they would like a special treat. They could fly out with the worker bees to gathered nectar. The children all looked at Ramor, and he nodded his head yes, so they nodded their heads yes. The procession of worker bees was forming, and off they flew out of the hive in search of bountiful flowers. Sometimes it took as many as twenty thousand trips to a field to make one pound of honey.

Flowers

Off they flew with their little transparent bees' wings just flapping away. There was a total of about five hundred honeybees, with the four children buzzing away right in the middle of them. Ramor stayed back at the hive to catch up on his rest, because he knew the honeybees would take good care of Lisa, David, Stacy, and Karen. They flew high above the ground and buzzed among the trees, across a river, and finally arrived in a meadow filled with the most beautiful flowers. Not only do the bright colors attract the bees, but most of all, the sweet smell tells the bees that a flower is rich in nectar. Nectar is what the bees collect to make their honey. The children saw a flower they recognized, the honeysuckle, which grows on a vine. They buzzed over to it. There were just hundreds and hundreds of sweet-smelling honeysuckle flowers. Each child sat on the edge of a flower petal and began to investigate. From so close, the flower looked rather strange. They could reach down inside the flower with their hands and scoop out the nectar, which was deliciously sweet. They felt almost like honeybees buzzing from flower to flower and tasting the sweet nectar of the honeysuckle.

Suddenly there was a cry of "help!" The children looked around! There were Lisa, David, and Stacy, but where was Karen? There it was again—"Help! Help!" It was coming from a flower at the end of the vine. They flew over to it. Little Karen had fallen headfirst right down into the throat of a flower while reaching for its nectar. She was trapped upside down in the flower. There she was hanging onto the stamen, one of the long slender parts on the inside of the flower. She had not quite fallen all the way in. Her little wings were flapping away, but to no avail. She was a funny sight to see, and the children had to laugh when they saw her. David grabbed one leg, Stacy grabbed the other, and Lisa held her around her waist. They counted, "One, two, three," and then they all pulled together. Well, did she ever come out, and fast! It was like pulling a cork out of a bottle. There was even a loud pop, and down they fell onto the grass below. Everyone was fine.

Karen sniffled a little and said, "Not funny." Then she, too, started to laugh.

Next, they flew over to the daffodils that were bright yellow and had a wonderful fragrance. The daffodils had nice long leaves sprouting out of the ground that appeared to make wonderful sliding boards. David flew up to the top of a leaf and came sliding back down. He slid down the leaf like a rocket.

He said, "I felt just like one of my Hot Wheels cars."

Then they all had to give it a try. Of course, since they had little wings, their feet never hit the ground. When they came sliding down to the bottom, they would just zoom into the air and fly back to the top of the long slender green leaf.

After a while they decided to find the rest of the bees, who had been concentrating on a field of tall white daisies. The bees needed to gather as much nectar as they could to make enough honey to last the coming winter. This would be the food that would sustain the entire bee colony throughout the cold winter months when no flowers were in bloom. It takes about four hundred to five hundred pounds of honey for them to live during this period. That's why when you see the honeybee, he is always busily buzzing around the flowers and doesn't have much time for play. (The bees are cousins to the ants, who are also very hard workers.)

The bees must be careful where they build their homes. They are usually high up in a tree, out of the reach of bears. The bears just love that delicious bee honey but are a nuisance to the bees. Fortunately, in this neck of the woods, the bees didn't have to worry much about raiding bears.

In the distance it looked like dark storm clouds were gathering, so the worker bee leader gave the signal to head for home. Buzz, buzz, buzz over the valley, across the river, and high into the trees they flew. In just a little while they were back at the hive. Ramor was there to greet them. They told him about little Karen's fall into the flower, and they all laughed once again. The queen came out and provided cake and honey for them to eat before they returned home.

The honey was delicious and nourishing. It was just what they needed for the long flight back. They thanked the queen bee, and she told them they were welcome to visit her colony any time.

In no time, they had all flown back to the old oak tree. In the blink of an eye, their wings had disappeared and so had Ramor.

"I guess it's time for us to go home," said Lisa. "The sun is starting to quickly set."

They sang merry songs as they walked down the path toward home.

That night as their mom tucked them in, she said, "I've got a surprise for you for breakfast!"

The next morning they rushed into the kitchen, eager to see the surprise. Mom had fixed them nice, hot biscuits, and there on the table beside the plate of biscuits was a large jar of honey for them to pour over their biscuits.

"How did you know we liked honey?" Lisa asked.

Their mom replied, "Oh, a little bee told me!"

The Raft

Now that school was back in session the children weren't able to spend as much time playing outside as they had in the summertime so they made good use of each Saturday. The weather was still warm, and it seemed almost like summer, but the flowers were starting to disappear, and the first signs of fall were about. The leaves were beginning to turn color, and there was a slight nip in the air. All four children were up bright and early this particular Saturday morning and were anxious to go out into the fresh morning sunshine to begin their day. Lisa suggested they pack a lunch and head down the path into the woods for a nice picnic. They had never gone past the tree where they always met their friend Ramor, so they decided to do a little exploring farther down the path and find a good spot for a picnic.

They helped Mom with the picnic lunch and packed everything in a straw basket that had been in the hall closet just waiting for such an occasion. Before long everything was in order for the picnic, and off they went down the winding path into the woods. Once they entered the woods the air was cool and fresh, because the tall trees shaded them from the sun. Soon the path paralleled the little creek that led them to their special spot. Every now and then they would see a small fish swimming by or a little crayfish skimming along the sandy bottom. David and the girls wished they had a jar with them so they might try to catch a few crayfish and take them back home. They thought they would someday return to this spot and give it a try.

Soon they came upon their old oak tree, but they kept going farther down the path to explore what was beyond. The path still followed beside the little stream. They came to a beautiful clearing. They noticed that here the stream fed into a much larger river that they had not seen before. Under the trees beside the meadow and on the bank beside the stream would be the perfect place for their picnic.

While the girls were getting the lunch out of the basket, David did a little more exploring on his own, walking along the shoreline of the large river. It was fun walking beside the river, and he was being careful not to get his new tennis shoes wet.

After a while, he came upon a small cave that was almost hidden from view by tall bushes. There was a little sandy beach in front of the cave and resting in the middle of the beach was an old log raft. It must have been there for years. It was rather weather-beaten, and the lashings were broken in several places. He was excited to find it in this secret hideaway and ran back to tell the girls about his discovery. He arrived back just in time. Lisa was getting ready to call him for lunch. He told her about the raft while he ate his sandwich. He told her that perhaps they could repair the raft and float it away from the cave he had discovered. Whoever had built it originally had probably forgotten all about it by now.

They finished eating their lunch and had delicious homemade brownies for dessert. Mom had put in a thermos of lemonade for them to drink, and it, too, was delicious. They folded up the tablecloth on which they had been eating and packed up everything in the picnic basket. Lisa carried the lunch basket with her, and down along the river they ran to look at the raft David had discovered.

Soon they came upon the hidden cave, and there was the raft on the beach where David had discovered it.

Lisa said, "Do you think we might repair it and see if we can get it to float? Let's go over and take a look."

When they got beside the raft, they thought it best to take their shoes and socks off so they wouldn't get them wet. All four children sat down on a big rock and removed their shoes and placed them neatly upon the top of the rock. They then raced down the sandy beach toward the raft. When they looked more closely at the raft, they saw that all it really needed was for the logs to be tied together more securely. That presented a problem, because they had no rope or string with them. David did have his pocketknife handy and decided to strip the bark from some young poplar trees standing nearby. He had read in one of his schoolbooks how the Indians had done this and used the bark to lash logs together to make shelters. While he was doing this, the girls splashed in the shallow water. The sandy bottom felt good between their toes.

In no time David was back, and they got to work with their project of fixing up the raft. It was hard work binding the logs together, but they did the best job they knew how. Once they were finished, it was time to push the raft into the water to test its seaworthiness. Lisa, David, Stacy, and Karen pushed as hard as they could. The raft finally began to slide and went skidding into the water with a tremendous splash. They kept their fingers crossed that it would float. It disappeared from view as it crashed into the water. They hoped it would come back up.

Down the River

Would the raft sink or float? They waited and watched. Sure enough it returned to the surface, and they all cheered. David waded out to the raft and pushed it back onto the shore. He tied a rope securely around one of the logs and set a large rock on the rope so the raft couldn't drift away. The children thought it would be great fun to take a ride on the raft. The water in the river was very shallow. It was deep enough for the raft to float but still shallow enough for the children to stand in. Lisa picked up the picnic basket, and, taking their shoes and socks with them, they jumped onto the raft. David was last aboard and shoved the raft out into the current; then he jumped aboard. As they floated along, Stacy and Karen sat in the middle of the raft while David and Lisa stood near the edge watching the water and rocks passing by. In one corner of the raft was a pile of canvass all neatly bundled. They had not paid much attention to it before. Lisa went to investigate and untied the ropes that bound it together. Meanwhile, David was keeping the raft free of rocks and entanglements by guiding the raft with a long pole he had brought along from shore.

All at once Lisa shouted, "David, Stacy, Karen, look what I've found!"

They rushed over to see. The canvas, which had been neatly rolled up, turned out to be a small tent.

Lisa said, "Why don't we try to put up the tent on the raft so we'll have a shelter in case of rain." (There were a few dark clouds coming up on the horizon.)

There were two center poles for the tent. After much coaxing and explaining, Lisa got Stacy to hold one pole and Karen to hold the other while Lisa and David pulled the tent tightly over the poles. Stacy and Karen were inside the tent, and Lisa and David were tying it down to the logs on the sides of the raft. It only took them a few minutes to get the tent up, but they had to untie it in several places to pull it tighter and then retie it to the logs. When everything was finished, they opened the front flap and threw it back over the side of the tent. They crawled inside and were excited about the cozy little nest that they had put together. Lisa brought the picnic basket inside the tent and, since they had worked so hard, they decided it was time for a snack. They sat in the tent enjoying some cookies and lemonade that they had saved from lunch. It was so peaceful just sitting there floating down the river.

The water in the river was very clear, and every now and then the children would see a fish swim by the raft. Lisa thought she would try her luck at catching one. She fashioned a hook out of an old piece of wire that she found binding one of the logs and then tied some stout string that David had discovered in his pocket on the long pole they had been using to guide the raft. She sat on the edge of the raft dangling her feet in the water, holding the fishing pole. She tied a piece of chicken onto the hook with a piece of bright ribbon (using one of her own hair ribbons) in hopes that the fish would think that it looked like a tempting, delicious bug.

After a while the dark clouds they had seen in the distance began to get closer, and there was thunder and lightning in the sky. Then the rain came, and did it pour! They sure were lucky to have erected the tent. They crawled inside where they stayed nice and dry. With all the rain, the current in the stream moved them faster and faster, and they were having quite a merry ride. The raft would go this way and that as they swiftly went along their way. The rain shower passed in a hurry, and then there was a beautiful rainbow in the sky that signaled the end of the storm. The sky was clear and blue once again.

About that time there was a "bump, bump." They had run aground. There was a line of rocks jutting out into the stream that was blocking their way. Lisa and David hopped off of the raft and used the rope to tow it to the shoreline, which wasn't far away. After they secured the raft, they thought it would be best to leave the raft where it was and head for home since it was almost dinnertime and their mom would be wondering what was keeping them. They tied the raft's rope securely around a tree and covered the raft with foliage so it would be well hidden. They would keep the raft here so they could come back and take another ride some other time. It was going to be fun to have their secret raft anchored at their secret hiding place. They carefully took the tent down and rolled it up. Before they left, they made sure no one could see the raft from the path from above the stream. When all looked secured, the four children held hands and climbed the hill from the stream to the path that led toward home. They could see their old oak tree in the far distance and followed the path back toward it. It really had been a fun day, and a day that they could do all over again whenever they wanted, because they had their own private raft. Off they went, homeward bound to see their beautiful mother once again.

Pumpkins

Fall was in the air. The nights were getting chilly, and the grass was covered with frost early in the mornings. All the children in the neighborhood had to wear jackets in the morning to school but usually carried them home in the afternoon over their shoulders while enjoying the warming sunshine. They were getting excited about Halloween, which was approaching. Soon the big night would be here. Lisa, David, Stacy, and Karen were thinking about what costumes they would wear on their Halloween night rounds. Lisa had already been a gypsy, so she didn't want to be that again. Stacy thought she might like to dress up as a gypsy this year, with plenty of lipstick and rouge on her face and a long dress and a bandanna covering her hair.

David had already been a tiger, and this year he thought that being a pirate would be just perfect after his recent pirate adventure with Ramor. He would look for a black patch to wear over one eye and would need a sword to wear at his waist. He had several long sticks and thought perhaps he could fashion a sword out of one of them. If he could only persuade his mom to cut up an old pair of trousers (sort of jagged around the bottom), then he would be all set. He didn't like the idea of wearing an earring in one ear. He thought he would find a picture of a pirate in the library just to be sure he knew how they dressed.

Karen wanted to be a clown again this year, and Stacy's costume from last year was a perfect fit for her. Stacy was happy to let her wear it. Lisa had a brilliant idea! She would go as a pumpkin—a Halloween pumpkin, a jack-o-lantern. She would get busy right away making her costume. She wasn't exactly certain how she would do it. She would make a great big orange ball and then cut it out like a jack-o-lantern; her body would be inside with her head and arms sticking out of the top and sides. She knew that if she could fashion such a costume, no one would recognize her. This would be her project to work on between now and October 31.

David volunteered to tell everyone his Halloween joke. He asked, "Does anyone know what they call a hot dog without any meat in it?"

All the girls were silent.

"A hollow weenie!" he exclaimed.

No one laughed.

"Oh well," he said, "it was a good try."

Lisa said it was really a very clever joke, and he should tell it to the children in school.

Later that afternoon Mother came back from the grocery store and had a surprise with her for the children. She had bought a great big pumpkin for the children to carve, with her help, into a Halloween jack-o-lantern. She even had a big candle to place inside when it was finished. She left it on the dining room table and thought they would work on it later in the week. At supper that night, the pumpkin was the main topic of conversation. Everyone wondered how it would look when they completed carving it. They were eager to put it in a window at night with a lighted candle inside. Right now, though, the pumpkin just maintained its place of honor in the center of the family dining room table.

That night, the children went to bed with pleasant thoughts of all the fun they were going to have on Halloween night and all the delicious candy they were going to collect. Soon they were fast asleep, but at that very moment, something strange was going on in the family living room.

Happy Endings

There they were, about a dozen pumpkins dancing around in a circle in the living room and making quite a racket. But they weren't exactly pumpkins. Each one had a happy jack-o-lantern face and was glowing mischievously in the dark.

They awakened the children! When the pumpkins saw the children, they stopped their dancing and had a look on their carved faces like they were caught doing something they shouldn't.

One of the pumpkins, a big fat one, waddled up to the children and said, "Won't you come in? We were just practicing our Halloween dance! We didn't expect anyone to see us since it isn't even Halloween."

All four children came into the living room and sat on the floor and watched the pumpkins continue their dance. Soon a little pumpkin waltzed over and grabbed Lisa by the hand, and, before she knew it, she was in the middle of the circle with the pumpkins dancing around her.

Next came David, then Stacy, and finally Karen. All four of them were in the center while the pumpkins gaily danced around them. The children joined in by clapping their hands to the rhythm of the dancing. Everyone was laughing and having such a good time that it was a while before anyone heard the "tap-tap-tap" at the sliding glass door in the living room. Lisa went over to the door, pulled the curtain back, and looked out. She was so surprised at what she saw that she could hardly speak.

The pumpkin came over and said, "Don't be frightened. Those are just some of my friends who came over to practice for Halloween fun!"

Mr. Pumpkin had some interesting friends—a witch, a ghost, a pirate, and a gypsy lady. He opened the door and in they came, right into the living room. The ghost was sort of a smoky looking figure but had a smile on his face as he glided about the room. He had come through the door before it was even opened.

The old witch was not too frightening, and she stayed to herself most of the time. Once she offered Lisa a nice rosy, red apple, but Lisa turned it down. The witch spent most of her time flying around the dining room on her broomstick. She was a little rusty on sharp turns and bumped into the wall.

Now, the pirate looked a little familiar. The children remembered that he was the same pirate who had taken them on a search for buried treasure in their first adventure with Ramor. He gave each child a golden coin and told them to save it for a rainy day.

Last but not least was the gypsy lady. She was young and beautiful with dark eyes and long, black hair. She wore a white blouse and dark skirt covered with bright flowers. She held a crystal ball in her hand, because she was also a fortune-teller. She gathered the children around, so they could look into the crystal ball and see the future. As they gazed into the crystal ball, they saw three beautiful, young girls—each had long hair and graceful figures. They looked very familiar—why, it was Lisa, Stacy, and Karen, but now they were grown up. Then there was a tall, handsome young man behind them who turned out to be their brother, David.

How fine they had turned out to be. Their parents would be very proud of them. Then the crystal ball started to become hazy, and they could hardly see anything at all. Suddenly the figure of a happy, roly-poly man began to appear. Why, it was Ramor, their old friend, whom they hadn't seen in some time. He began to get bigger and bigger and bigger. All of a sudden, he popped right out of the crystal ball and was standing there in the living room.

He looked around and said, "What a grand time everyone is having!"

The pumpkins were dancing; the ghost and witch were flying around. The pirate was observing everything with a parrot on one shoulder, and the gypsy was smiling, as she could foretell the happy future that lay in store for Lisa, David, Stacy, and Karen.

"Children," Ramor said, "we have had some wonderful adventures together. Soon your father will return home from the war to look after you and your beautiful mother, and I know that you will have more exciting times together. I will leave you now to take other little children to see the strange and wonderful sights that you have seen.

"Remember, if you ever need me, just come down the path by the stream to our old oak tree and call my name. You four children will be my friends forever! Your dad will be home safely next week. Now, isn't that a happy ending to all our adventures?"

With that, Ramor vanished, and all the happy Halloween characters vanished with him. The children felt so sleepy that they fell asleep right there on the living room floor. The next morning their mom found them still asleep.

"Don't tell me that you children slept all night on the living room floor!"

"Yes, we did," they replied.

"I thought I told you children not to tell me that," their mom joked. "OK, let's get ready for breakfast."

Mom went over to the dining room table and saw the pumpkin, now carved with a wonderful jack-o-lantern face. It smiled up at her.

"Did you children stay up all night carving the face on that pumpkin?" she asked. "You did an excellent job. Why, it's so real that I thought it smiled at me."

Lisa, David, Stacy, and Karen just looked at each other and winked! Some day they would tell their mom about the wonderful Halloween party they had last night in her very own living room.

The End.

December 1984
Lisa, twenty-three; David, twenty-one; Karen, fifteen; and Stacy, seventeen.

EPILOGUE

April 15, 2007

Now, the four little children are all happily married and have families of their own!

Lisa is married to Ross and has two boys and a girl: Sam, age eleven; Arielle, age nine; and Davis, age five. They live in Orlando, Florida.

David is married to Jeanie and has three girls: Anne, age twelve; Sarah, age nine; Samantha, age six months. They live in Atlanta, Georgia.

Stacy is married to Robert and has two boys: Austin, age four; and Benjamin, age three. They live in Dublin, Ireland.

Karen is married to Michael and has two girls: Grace, age six; and Hope, age two. They live in Ponte Vedra, Florida.

And they all lived happily ever after!

ABOUT THE AUTHOR

Larry Michalove was born in 1933 and was raised in Asheville, North Carolina. He is a 1955 graduate of the United States Military Academy and later received a Master of Science degree from Stanford University. He resides in Birmingham, Alabama, with his wife of forty-seven years, Sybil. They have four children and ten grandchildren.

978-0-595-34799-5
0-595-34799-1